D0931443

Montraville

Episodes in an Early Appalachian Life

RON GRISWOLD

WITH A STORY BY JANE WEAVER

ISBN: 978-1-62429-426-6

Published through Opus Self-Publishing
Politics and Prose Bookstore
5015 Connecticut Ave. NW
Washington, D.C. 20008
www.politics-prose.com / / (202) 364-1919

Looking out over the mountains of Western North Carolina, the scenery is far grander than any I ever before beheld. Such an ocean of wooded, waving, swelling mountain grandeur is not to be described, all curves and slopes of inimitable softness and beauty. Oh, these forest gardens! What perfection, what divinity, in their architecture! What simplicity and mysterious complexity of detail!

—JOHN MUIR, *A Thousand-Mile Walk to the Gulf*

Table of Contents

Settlers Featured in This Narrative

Some dates are uncertain

WEAVER FAMILY
John Weaver (1763-1830) in 1785 married Elizabeth Biffle (ca.1773-1843)
Their Sons:

> Jacob Weaver (1786-1868) and his sons John Siler (1812-1875) and
> James Thomas (1828-1864)
> James Weaver (1794-1854) and his son Rufus (1829-1876)
> John "Jack" Weaver (1802-1838)
> Christopher "Chrisly" Weaver (1805-1843)
> Michael Montraville Weaver (1808-1882) in 1829 married Jane
> Eliza Baird (1810-1899)

The children of Montraville and Jane:

> James C Fulton Weaver (1837-1862)
> John Weaver (1839-1890)
> William Elbert "Will" Weaver (1841-1935)
> Mary Ann Weaver (1830-1890) in 1851 married James Americus
> Reagan (1824-1910)

BAIRD FAMILY
Brothers Bedent Baird (1767-1839) and Zebulon Baird (1764-1824)

> Bedent married Jane Welch. Their daughter is Jane Eliza Baird Weaver
> Zebulon's daughter Elmira "Mira" Margaret Baird (1802-1878) in
> 1825 married David Vance (1792-1844)

VANCE FAMILY
Brothers David Vance and Robert Brank Vance (1793-1827)
David and Mira's sons:

> Gov. and Col. Zebulon Baird Vance (1830-1894) and Gen. Robert
> Brank Vance (1828-1899)

Montraville

EPISODES IN AN EARLY APPALACHIAN LIFE

1

"Let There Be White"

Wherever one looked there were signs of spring. The snows, which had fallen heavily throughout the early part of 1787, had retreated to small patches beyond the reach of the sun. There was green everywhere, seemingly overnight. Crabapple trees were displaying their dainty white and pink blossoms. Wake-robins were beginning to point their flowers skyward. All kinds of woodpeckers, including the great crested, could be heard drumming, marking their territory. Ruffed grouse were fanning their wings and strutting about in an attempt to attract a mate. Bobwhite quail could be heard whistling their name. Countless wild pigeon nests weighed down branches almost to the breaking point. And the countryside looked so fine that John and Elizabeth Weaver would often just stop and stare, awestruck at the wonder of it all.

But the temperature was falling and thick gray clouds had, in an instant, camouflaged the setting sun. What had begun as a pleasant, albeit laborious, climb up into the Bald Mountains had become a footslog. John thought his family would be safe negotiating the mountains in April, and everything had gone smoothly up to that point, but now he was concerned. Had he made a mistake? He had battled the Redcoats and Loyalists years before and had traversed the Allegheny Mountains and the Shenandoah Valley, but that was with his capable and experienced brothers or on his own. Now he had a wife and child that needed his protection and he most definitely did not know this territory.

Elizabeth was willing and eager, and had shown considerable strength and resilience during the journey. But while she knew what was needed to keep the boy safe from harm, she was, after all, little more than a child herself. The safety of their six-month-old son Jacob was John's responsibility, first and foremost. And if the storm, and there would certainly be a storm, was a bad one, their situation was precarious.

A pack horse carried all their worldly goods, though they didn't amount to much. In addition to salt and food and a few articles of clothing, they had brought along an iron kettle, an axe, a butcher knife, some farming tools, and a couple of quilts. The little beast was game, well-trained, and with a sweet disposition, but he needed rest just as much if not more than they did. And the Indian trail was difficult to follow in the worsening light and would be impossible in snow.

Even more worrying was the fact that on top of Big Bald, at over 5,000 feet, there was little shelter. The trees had mostly disappeared and there stretched before them a wide, open space with tufts of mountain oat grass and wavy hairgrass, thick shrubs at its edges, and a spruce-fir stand some distance away. John had been advised that he would encounter such leas in the mountains, grassy balds they were called, but he had shrugged off the possibility that they would cause any significant disorientation. Now, however, it was clear that pressing on risked losing the trail completely or becoming trapped in the open in a snowstorm.

Scanning the terrain, Elizabeth asked: "Johnny, what are we goin' to do? We cain't go much futher can we?"

John, perhaps showing more confidence than he possessed, replied: "Don't fret Flittermouse, we have gone all the far we can today and I don't like the look of them clouds. I'll find us a spot where we can bed down. See the bushes over yonder? Let's head there."

Elizabeth was both relieved and, at the same time, somewhat dismayed by her husband's use of the strange endearment. She did not like to think that she had any bat-like qualities. But John had explained on the day he proposed that she reminded him of one of those spooky creatures, given her tendency to flit about, and that his father, who had been born in Germany and later settled in Holland, had sometimes called his mother Fleddermuys.

And she had to acknowledge that she did flit about. Why not? She was young and exuberant, and seemed to have the energy of three people. She could only hope that it was that, and not her swept-back, black-as-coal hair, which she kept shiny with the bear fat oil she always carried with her, and her slightly too prominent ears, that made John think of her in bat-like terms. Certainly she thought of herself more a butterfly or hummingbird.

Two years before, John had turned up in the Watauga Settlement at Sycamore Shoals, having been deflected from a trip to the Ohio Country with his brothers by the tales a comrade had told him during their service together in the War of Independence. Jacob Biffle had spoken of the lush, virtually empty (save for a handful of reputedly docile Injuns) land down south and of the lovely, growing-up-fast Elizabeth, all alone and supposedly pining to escape her lot in the backwoods. John was seeking a pretty bride and he wanted to settle down and start a family.

Elizabeth was initially uninterested. She was a raven-haired little beauty with a turned-up nose and piercing hazel eyes, a bit on the scrawny side but starting to flower into womanhood. She enjoyed the freedom and the lack of responsibility she had in her community. She was, after all, ten years younger than John who, especially considering his experiences, and experience, must have seemed even older. On the other hand, she yearned to get away and have an adventure. And John's stories of the war, in which he told of witnessing General George Washington at Monmouth Courthouse rallying the troops, and Molly Pitcher stepping in to man her husband's gun when he became incapacitated, were enthralling.

Elizabeth had no emotional ties to the area. In fact, she was bored much of the time. Yes, she was fond of animals both on the farm and in the forest. She loved to go walking on Lynn Mountain and in the summer go skinny dipping in the Blue Hole. And she adored dancing to fiddle music and listening to ballads such as "Barbara Allen." But she had no close companions and there was no school. There was a Presbyterian church which her relations attended, formed five years earlier by the Reverend Samuel Doak, but in all honesty she was not much of a churchgoer. And you would not say that she was religious.

However, John *was*. And while his obvious interest in young Elizabeth sparked much gossip, he made a favorable impression on Reverend Doak and the congregants with his knowledge of Scripture and talk about how God had looked after him and the whole Continental Army throughout the war. Furthermore, he was most assuredly handsome, with rugged good looks, and he was tall, with close to uncomfortably gorgeous blond hair. Into the bargain, he was clever and he had big plans. And Elizabeth's brother, tasked by their parents with looking after her, was keen on getting his sister settled, and preferably at some distance. He loved his little sister, no one could doubt that, but he had no interest in keeping an eye on her.

John wooed her with talk of a new life in a verdant, unspoiled spot with fertile soil for farming and livestock grazing. He promised her that he would see to her education. She did have a passion for learning and knew stories from the Bible, but could neither read nor write with any facility.

It did not hurt that John was, like her, of German ancestry. But the final test was – would he, could he, dance? And he passed, although in his case perhaps it would be closer to the truth to call what he did bumbling, rather than dancing. Still, he was willing to try and eventually Elizabeth was won over.

They were married in the summer of 1785 in Elizabeth's home, with her father Johannes giving her away (with, it must be said, some relief) and her mother quietly sobbing throughout the ceremony.

Elizabeth's simple Irish linen dress had been chosen to be of day-to-day use wherever the couple eventually settled down. But her brother had prettied it up with a bunch of bird-foot violets. John had on his best clothes, which were actually a bit shabby, but were spanking clean (Elizabeth had seen to that).

Following the ceremony there was a party the likes of which what was then Wayne County had seldom seen, with much singing and fiddle-playing and of course whiskey. While the older set seemed happy with drinking and tale-swapping, the younger set formed rings and played kissing games to songs such as "Old Sister Phoebe," games that Elizabeth had been the center of only a few weeks before. But now she was saving her kisses for John.

Elizabeth, radiant in her girlish youth and bonniness, was as excited and at the same time as fearful as any bride would be under the circumstances. She was not a complete innocent. After all, she had been born and raised on the frontier. But on the other hand, outside of pitching in with the farm work and helping her mother in the kitchen, she had had little of what one might consider worldly experience. Fortunately, her mother Catherine and elder sister Mary had taken her aside and explained a few things.

She may well have had doubts about taking a husband who was much older and infinitely more knowledgeable in all facets of life. But on their wedding night John was tender and gentle. They embraced and kissed for what seemed like an eternity, John assuring her that everything would be fine, that he would not do anything she didn't want him to do. And she did, eventually, open up to him.

It was certainly painful. John asked if he should stop, but in answer Elizabeth grasped his body and pulled him closer. There would be no climax for her, but she felt the first faint rumblings of future possibilities. And it did seem that the couple had been made for each other, enjoying increasingly happy relations as Elizabeth found that she had a keenness for physical lovemaking that meshed nicely with that of her husband.

Elizabeth knew she would have no control over where her future lay. The area was the center of the land that North Carolina had ceded to the new U.S. government in 1784 and then taken back due to mistrust of what the Congress of the Confederation would do.

A group of prominent citizens, convinced that Congress would dither and that they would receive no protection from the U.S. or North Carolina, had met in Jonesborough. There they formed a new state, the State of Franklin (or Frankland, depending on whom you talked to). A constitution was drafted, containing such sensible provisions as barring from office-holding anyone of immoral character, as well as ministers, attorneys and doctors. In short, all the requisites of a government – courts, political jurisdictions, taxes, civil employees, even treaties with the Indians – were in place.

It wasn't lawless; instead, two sets of laws were being enforced at the same time. This did not sit well with John or his father-in-law, who was relieved when North Carolina reasserted its jurisdiction. But by that time John and Elizabeth were awaiting the birth of their son Jacob. And soon thereafter they were away, following their dream.

And now here they were with their child, in the middle of nowhere, with no certain destination, with no shelter, and with a snowstorm about to hit.

Jacob started wailing, Elizabeth wrapping him tighter in his blanket. But he was not to be appeased. He was tired, cold, and hungry. But at least he wasn't old enough to be scared. He could leave that to his parents.

Then, only a few yards away, Elizabeth sensed movement and cried out: "Johnny, somethin's movin' over by them bushes." Yes, but fortunately not Indians, and not a bear. They were wild hogs, grotesque creatures, of a size that might well spell trouble if they decided to attack. But the good news was that John and Elizabeth had found a spot that would be perfect for riding out the storm.

"I'll be durn'd! Them critters can smell folks and other animals from miles off and they tend to keep away from people whenever they can. Them bein' here and them stayin' here causes me to believe they know we are in for a bad'un and they surely do not want to leave their den. But they will. Razorbacks can barely see and they frighten easy. Don't worry pet," assured John, "they are afeard of us."

This was partly John demonstrating his confidence and partly him putting on a brave front. He well knew that the hogs had a hide as tough as any leather and a pointy snout that could dig into the earth better than any spade and, he was fairly certain, dig into a man or woman just as easily. But time was of the essence and like a madman he ran straight at the group, which appeared to be bedding down for the night, and they scattered in all directions, vacating a den that looked for all the world as warm and soft as a feather bed. It appeared that the hogs had dug themselves into a patch of thick catawba rosebay, protected on three sides and padded with long-dead leaves and moss.

Now that the hogs had been expelled, a fire was needed, and quickly, to make sure they kept their distance.

"Liz, this here ain't ideal, but if them hogs felt safe my thinkin' is that it'll suit us. Now I'm fixin' to gather up some firewood. There'll be no roarin' blaze, but maybe two or three little fires around our cozy den."

This was no easy task, for the woods on the edge of the clearing were sparse. And the couple certainly did not want to wander far. Fortunately, there were some scraggly pines not too distant. Elizabeth helped as best she could while carrying a crying baby and was able, with some difficulty, to gather a handful of twigs, sticks, pine needles, and bark. She even discovered dry punk, excellent tinder, inside some rotting logs. John went farther into the brush, still keeping an eye on Elizabeth and their den should the hogs return, and was able to gather up enough kindling and branches to at least get them through the night.

In short order, John had his flint and steel out, and was hard at work starting a fire.

"Johnny, you has to teach me how to do that! It seems almost like magic!"

"The trick is to put the flint as close as you can to the tinder and char and strike downwards with the steel. And try to hit the center of the char dead on. Then, when you see a little smoke, blow on it whilst you add more tinder. Before you know it, there's a flame....well, maybe not before you know it. Let's try that again."

Highly proficient from his service in the war and his later journeys, and with a sharp-edged flint, a well-tempered steel, and a dry char cloth, under normal circumstances John would have had little trouble starting a fire. But the snow was beginning to fall in earnest. Still, after enlisting Elizabeth's help in shielding the tinder, John had three small fires going on the edge of their improvised sleeping quarters and the couple could begin to anticipate if not a pleasant night at least an endurable one, without the presence of wild hogs.

While John, who seemed to have a miraculous ability to turn simple and unpromising materials into whatever was required, set out to convert the hogs' bed into a shelter fit for his family, Elizabeth tended to Jacob. Her milk was thick and creamy. She took great pains to maintain as healthy a diet as possible. That had been easy back home, but on the trail it was becoming ever more difficult.

They had pemmican made from deer meat, as well as hardtack, parched corn, and pumpkin leather, and that blessed beverage coffee would be available as soon as the fire cooperated. They were well-stocked, which was fortunate because even before the snow, with the exception of a few early wild berries and acorns, food along the trail had been hard to come by. But John had been able to harvest a couple of wild turkeys and of course the beautiful, meaty pigeons, so numerous in the pine forests that he didn't even have to use his rifle on them. Rocks or sticks were all that was required.

Thus Elizabeth could not but wonder why John had not taken a shot at the fleeing hogs. His answer: "I been askin' myself the same question. Though I weren't sure there were time to get the flintlock ready, and firin' is never a sure thing, and gettin' them hogs to disappear seemed of immediate importance. But don't fret -- if'n they return, my fusil will be ready."

After getting the fire going, John worked at fashioning a rudimentary lean-to. A couple of boughs cut from a scrawny tree with his axe provided additional shelter overhead and the packs removed from the horse formed a frontal barrier. The unfortunate animal was now left mostly to its own devices. In the snow and cold, he was not about to lie down. However, John found a spot somewhat protected from the wind, and pulled out an extra quilt for the poor beast. So the whole family was as snug as possible in such a difficult situation. The snow was now falling heavily and the wind was picking up. But with the fires, and curling up together, the threesome was reasonably content. In any event, there was nothing to do but try to sleep. Jacob, fortunately, after his meal managed the task without difficulty.

"You have such an amazin' knack for calmin' that child, Flittermouse," said John. "Will he grow up to be your opposite?"

Elizabeth, still anxious and on the watch for any hogs that wanted their bed back, but also exceedingly tired, replied: "If you mean, will the lad not bounce around like me, that I cain't say. The only thing I am certain of is that he will make us proud and continue to fill us with joy."

Then shortly thereafter, sleep overtook her and even John, although he woke frequently to tend the fires. At one point in the early morning, with the snow still falling at a rapid clip, he shook himself awake to find Elizabeth staring at him.

"Johnny, tell me again about where we'uns is headin'? Will this be worth it? Will we be safe? Will we be happy thar?"

John had answered these questions before of course. He often had to remind himself that Elizabeth was still amazingly young, with nothing like his knowledge of the world, and with a child that depended on her. There might be times when he could joke about their situation or pass her concerns off as nothing to worry about. But he knew she was uneasy, and rightly so. This was no time to treat her disquiet lightly.

"We will be happy wherever it is we settle down. That I promise you. I have loved you since the first moment I seen you and whilst I know you needed some convincin' about me, I do now believe you are comin' to love me. And we will be safe. I got myself through the war with nary a scratch and tromped mile after mile to find you. You, and Jacob of course, won't never have cause to doubt my commitment to your welfare. I allow that it will not always be easy. However, I do firmly believe not just that this will all be worth it, but that our family will thrive and prosper in a land that will, with hard work and the help of the Almighty, the Author of our being, provide everything we could possibly want and need.

"We will build a fine house, have bounteous harvests, see our sons and daughters grow up to be outstanding citizens of this new country. All our young'uns will know their letters. So will you! Our station will be amongst the highest in the land. We will have intercourse with other settlers and mayhap even with Injuns, who I have learned in my travels are not, all of 'em, the savages many consider them. I won't rest till we has discovered just the right place, and I know we will find it. Maybe not tomorrow -- all right, definitely not tomorrow -- but not all that far off.

"I've heard remarkable things about the lands in the Blue Ridge, and that is where we will make our home. When we find a good spot...." But then he noticed that his young wife had fallen fast asleep. He didn't credit himself with an especially soothing voice or manner of speech, but if she were half as tired as he was, he marveled that she could have been awake at all. So he tended to the fires as best he could, and closed his eyes for another nap.

For him especially it was a long night. The snow continued to fall until near dawn, more snow than John had seen since he left Pennsylvania. But on the plus side, it meant there was less chance of the family being surprised by any person or animal intent on making mischief. As long as the hogs (maybe even with reinforcements) did not return.

By first light the snow had stopped and the day showed some promise of being a clear one. The view from the grassy bald of the surrounding hills was something neither John nor Elizabeth would ever forget. It was as if God had tired of the verdant slopes and valleys, the lush trees, bushes, and grasses and said: "Let there be white!"

The pair stared in stunned amazement at the scene all around them. Nonetheless, John and Elizabeth were more than ready to be off again, if the way could be found under the thick blanket of fresh snow.

"Pet, why don't you fix us up somethin' to eat whilst I look yonder for the trail?"

"Be happy to, Johnny, and be happier still to get us outta here, but I'd better tend to Jakey first."

If the trail was to be found, it would be through the grassy area that dominated the top of the mountain, which seemed to offer no clues as to how they should proceed. John set out with perhaps more hope than expectation, but he had done a lot of surveying in his time and he had a fine surveyor's compass. And he knew he wanted to head south, which was for the most part the way the well-established trail had been heading up to that point. It did appear that if he kept that heading there was a promising forested area a couple of hundred yards away. Sure enough, after much stumbling through the snow, grass, and bushes, he found what appeared to be a trail through the woods.

After returning to the campsite, he was pleased to be greeted with a hug and a cup of hot coffee. "I do believe I has found it. Anyhow, we ain't got a lot of choices. I ain't stayin' hereabouts any longer than necessary."

So they again set out. It would be several days before they found what they were looking for: available land along a creek, in the shadow of the Blue Ridge Mountains, in what would soon become Buncombe County. There, John and Elizabeth would make their home, worship, and flourish. And have ten more children, the last of whom, Montraville, is the hero of this story.

2

"Peaceful Intentions"

"That's the last, correct? John?"

So said Elizabeth after the birth of their eleventh child. "You wanted another son and you have him. And 'less I am quite mistaken, he shall do the both of us proud. So, no more!"

The midwife, Hannah, agreed. "Missus is too old now. This one were hard, hard for the both of us."

To which Elizabeth replied: "Beg pardon! Old? Well, the way I feel at this moment in time I is sorely tempted to agree with you. Certainly too old, I'll warrant, for another birthin' like this one."

John was tempted to make a joke about an even dozen, or maybe a baker's dozen, but Elizabeth was now 35 years old and had been bearing children for more than 20 years, and he was 45. He knew this had been a difficult pregnancy and, besides, they were now grandparents three times over. It was time to call it quits.

"Yes, indeed, I s'pose we doesn't have to replace ever' child who leaves the nest," said John, trying unsuccessfully to stifle a grin. "But are you really goin' to insist on that name? Montraville? I'll admit it has a certain ring to it, but I'd feel better if he weren't such a swine in that infernal *Charlotte Temple*. If only it had been a girl! I quite like the name Charlotte....Say, can't we try again?"

"The matter is closed. But I will settle for Michael as a first name if that will mollify you. Although I know what I shall be calling him.

"And as for John Montraville, he was not a swine," retorted Elizabeth. "He loved Charlotte and was true to her and it was only 'cause he was

15

betrayed by that so-called friend of his that ever'thin' turned out as it did. And besides, he avenged her death. And it's such an elegant, distinctive name. A name no one is likely to forget. Yes, Montraville it is. That is his name."

"If that's how you want it, that's fine with me. But it would make me truly happy if you kept that book someplace where he will never find it, and when he asks about his name, tell him.... Well, make somethin' up please." John did not usually get so worked up, and this anger was, in truth, largely feigned. He actually liked the name, if not the character in the book.

And as his parents had agreed, this child was the last. And as Elizabeth could not help thinking on more than one occasion, the best.

When John and Elizabeth had arrived at their spot along the creek 21 years earlier, they knew it was what they had been seeking, and so they immediately set about making a home. There were Catawba in the region, and a Cherokee village was well-established, perhaps had been there since the 15th century. That was when the Cherokee had traveled south from the Great Lakes, displacing other tribes and inhabiting a vast area of the southeastern mountains. There they had set up stable settlements, autonomous villages linked by a shared language, and an expansive trading network.

Along the creek there was plenty of room and John, having had some dealings with Indians on the frontier, knew their ways. He had a knack for communicating with them through a combination of gesturing, pointing, and smiling. A quick learner, he was able to pick up enough of the Cherokee tongue to assure them of his peaceful intentions, and enough of their customs to get started on establishing a homestead.

For his service in the War John had received a bounty land warrant from the Continental Congress, entitling him to 160 acres in the Northwest Territory. Using specie and currency from the transfer of his warrant to his brothers, and earned from the odd jobs he had performed as he made his way west and south after the war, he was able to purchase prime acreage on both sides of the creek and along a path leading to the French Broad River. Right away he began fashioning a wattle and daub residence, what the Cherokee called an *asi*, by weaving rivercane, wood, and vines into a frame, sealing it with a mixture of wet soil, clay and straw, and thatching the roof with grass.

Relations between the settlers and the Indians were in general amicable, although it was not always so. One day, what sounded like battle cries were heard, terrifying sounds that caused those working in the fields to immediately run for cover. John and a couple of neighbors, Adam Waggoner and Joseph Hughey, grabbed their firearms and took off in the direction the cries came from, the campsite of a Mr. Rims. He was a crotchety hunter, trapper, and would-be gold prospector who had been living alone near the creek.

Rims was not what you would consider a sociable fellow. On a couple of occasions his closest neighbors had sought him out and attempted to make conversation, and even invited him to share a meal with them. Their efforts were quickly rebuffed, Rims making it clear he did not welcome visitors.

"I thank ye kindly for comin', for it's little wage ye get by comin' t'see an ole man lak me. I doesn't value comp'ny and I has work to do. So if'n it is all the same to ye, please be gittin' along."

The message was received, loud and clear. There were those who thought that maybe, just maybe, Rims had found some of that elusive gold, and had no interest in taking a chance that his neighbors might try to horn in on his "treasure."

At any rate, no further attempt was made to connect with Mr. Rims until those apparent war cries were heard. When the trio arrived at his campsite, Rims and what they assumed were Indians were nowhere in sight. But there was a trail of blood leading toward a nearby cave. Approaching the cave with care, the party discovered the unfortunate Mr. Rims quite dead, scalped and pin-cushioned with arrows.

Whatever Mr. Rims had done to upset the Indians no one could say. Did they have blood on their minds? Perhaps they only wanted water for their horses or to powwow with him and the irascible recluse mistook their arrival as an attack. So he aggressively defended himself, which the Indians took exception to and did what they felt was appropriate.

The settlers raised the matter with their Cherokee acquaintances, who insisted that they knew nothing about it. Perhaps it had been a roving band of renegade *Ani ta gua* (Catawba) warriors that were not likely to be seen in the area again after what had happened. And indeed, they never were seen in the area after that. The unfortunate victim was then immortalized when the settlers started calling their watercourse Rims Creek.

Elizabeth's dealings with the Cherokee were initially awkward. After all, when she and John arrived she was still only 15 years old and had never had any interactions with them. One day, she had left Jacob asleep in their asi while John was working some distance away and paid a visit to a neighbor who, with her husband, had settled along the creek a few months before the Weavers. When she returned, Jacob's bed was empty. Rushing outside, she spotted a Cherokee brave holding the child. He pointed to a shirt Elizabeth had recently dyed a pretty color, drying in the sun near the hut.

Her first instinct was to race toward the man and try to wrestle the child away from him. But she was not, in fact, one to panic, and after thinking it through she realized that he wanted to exchange the baby for the shirt. She retrieved it, placed it halfway between the Indian and her hut and retreated to the entrance of the asi. Sure enough, the brave snatched up the garment and laid down the baby in its place. Later, Elizabeth heard a loud noise outside and, thinking John might have returned, peered out of the entrance only to find a freshly killed rabbit near the rock, and the same Indian running into the forest.

Was this simply a question of an Indian wanting some pretty cloth? Or was he trying to teach the young mother never to leave her child unattended? At any rate, that is certainly a lesson that Elizabeth learned.

Other lessons also needed to be mastered, although her time back home awaiting the birth of Jacob had been well spent in discovering some of what she needed to know. This included rudimentary kitchen and sewing skills learned from her mother. But with regard to the various capabilities needed to survive in what was little more than a wilderness, she was largely self-taught, although her neighbors, and the Cherokee after she got to know them better, helped a good deal.

She developed into a decent enough cook, despite the fact that she never could overcome her distaste for the slaughtering of birds both wild and domestic, especially the chickens that she raised herself. But needs must, and chickens made up a large part of the family's diet. Otherwise, John especially liked her bean dumplings, made of fine corn meal (much better after the new grist mill opened), wood ash lye, and of course cooked beans. He would eat them plain or with butter; it was all the same to him.

She became a more than passable seamstress and weaver of cloth. In the early days, flax fiber was used for weaving, but flax is extremely difficult, in terms of both time and effort, to grow and then turn into linen thread and, finally, cloth. Wool was somewhat less onerous, but it was cotton which eventually became the material of choice, especially after cotton thread became available in skeins. When their house was built, she insisted that there also be a side building where a loom could be placed. There Elizabeth produced the cloth needed for the ever-growing household's clothing and bed linens.

She learned basketry from the Indians, and became adept at making creels and bowls from the rivercane which grew in abundance along the banks of the creek and river. She mastered the art of dyeing the cane splinters black from the butternut tree and orange from bloodroot and was able to fashion designs. She prided herself especially on being able to turn out work so tight that it could hold water.

She enjoyed making corn shuck dolls for her daughters, using a whole green cob, hacking out a part where the neck would be, pulling it to the base, and tying it down. She then attached shucks for the arms and added some scraps of cloth to dress the dolls. The face remained blank since, according to Cherokee tradition, the figure's vanity would have caused the Almighty to steal it.

Elizabeth also learned pottery-making from the Indians, using the coiling method, in which clay, after the arduous process of sifting, cleaning, and mixing, was used to make a base and coils. The coils were then placed upon the base, one on top of each other, and smoothed, perhaps decorated, and finally fired, thus producing vessels of various sizes. When she became proficient, she was able to obtain colors and even patterns in her pottery through the use of different types of wood in the firing. Hardwoods, which smoked less, produced a light gray color, whereas softwoods such as poplar made the pieces darker.

She tended to her kitchen garden, growing corn, beans, cushaw squash and sunflowers, as well as plants for herbal medicines. She also learned from the Cherokee where she could gather the various medicinal herbs that grew throughout the region, including peppermint, chamomile, jewelweed, sassafras, hawkweed, and feverwort. Her favored remedies included blackberry root, which she made into a cordial to mitigate the effects of diarrhea, and extracts from dogwoods and wahoos to alleviate chills and fever.

It was a hard life and it never seemed to get easier. And what with caring for Jacob and the children who came with some regularity thereafter, cooking, milking the cow which John had obtained from one of the Cherokee, making clothes, doing the thousand and one chores that needed attending to, and simply keeping first the hut and later the house clean and dry, there was little time for the book learning Elizabeth had hoped for. But with John's help, she began to learn her letters through Bible study.

While Elizabeth was obtaining the many competencies she would need, John Weaver had two major endeavors in mind: replacing the hut with a real home and of course feeding his family. His first crop after clearing the land was the Cherokee staple, white eagle corn, which he was able to grow even on sloping land with painstaking attention to the shaving off of any plants sprouting up alongside the young corn stalks. He left the roots of the weeds to rot, thereby increasing the fertility of the soil. He soon was growing wheat, beans, turnips, and other vegetables, and then, after procuring a pair of slaves who taught him a thing or two, sorghum.

Later he would buy the first threshing machine in the area, but for years there was nothing but hand threshing, grueling work in which the entire family participated. John established a still for making brandy, although some years later this was shut down when, prompted by Methodist circuit riders, he took up the cause of temperance.

He raised cattle and hogs, and all sorts of fowl, and set about building a proper home.

One key task had been the establishment of a smithy, so he could make shoes for the horses he acquired, plowing implements, and, crucially, the five-inch long, thick nails needed for constructing a house from the wide planks he cut with his rip saw. Eventually, the forge would become a fully functioning blacksmith shop, with a large furnace and an enormous double-acting piston bellows in which air was blown out on both strokes of the handle.

John had learned the rudiments of blacksmithing up north, but along the creek, with the assistance of his neighbors, he became a true artist, able to fashion fine hunting knives as well as, to Elizabeth's delight, kitchen utensils, and tools such as the drawknives and spokeshaves essential to furniture-making. He was pleasantly surprised to discover that one of his slaves, Lucas, who was frankly not much good at farming, or house work for that matter, was a natural blacksmith.

John taught him the ancient hammer language of the anvil, how the sound made by hammer striking anvil varies according to the location of the hammer strike. Lucas quickly learned how he should hit the metal being fashioned based on the tone John was able to achieve. As they grew up, Jacob and the other boys also took up the peculiar art form, with Lucas taking the lead and John conducting. Elizabeth, in the kitchen, would often leave the door to the house open so she could listen to the music being "played" by John, Lucas, and the boys.

Lucas's skill was such that he was frequently hired out to neighbors, profiting both the household and Lucas, since the fees or barter were split. On occasion he was loaned out, thus creating good will with John's neighbors and even the Cherokee. Perhaps Lucas' greatest achievement was fashioning a splendid pipe tomahawk that John was pleased to be able to present to Chief Bowl, known in his language as Duwali, the most prominent Cherokee in the area. This did much to cement the bonds of friendship between the settlers and the Indians.

So, over the years a thriving farmstead was established, centered on a well-formed, hand-hewn, black locust-framed home, with a wooden ceiling and clapboarded walls, the first framed house in the area. There was a fireplace built with bricks made by John from the plentiful clay that was mixed with water, packed in molds, left to dry for several days, and then baked in his kiln. The fireplace had a baking and warming oven, and was wide and deep enough to accept large branches and logs. Even a bench could be accommodated, which the little ones vied with each other to occupy on the coldest days. And soon there was a shed with a corn-crib and granary, and a smokehouse where the hogs ended up, salt-cured and cold-smoked, hanging from the rafters for as much as a couple of years.

And slave quarters needed to be built. These crude earthen-floored log structures were daubed with clay in an attempt to keep out drafts and rain. There was a fireplace with a wooden chimney and a couple of shut-tered windows for ventilation. But there was no getting around the real-ity of the dirt floors, swept constantly by the women, and leaky roofs which seemed to forever be in a state of disrepair. It was always too cold or too hot. And every sort of pest found its way inside.

And of course the slaves led a life of tedious, back-breaking work and zero freedom. This was not plantation slavery, but even in Western North Carolina most slaves confronted brutality and denigration every day of their lives. Still, by the standards of the day, John's slaves were treated well, or at least that is how John viewed the matter. He was per-plexed by the offensive attitudes and harsh methods of some of his fellow slaveholders. He firmly believed that he was likely to get the most out of any person, and that included slaves, by providing more reward and less punishment. So his slaves had enough to eat and requisite clothing. And a patch of land where they could grow vegetables and raise some fowl.

Believing that religion taught respect for and obedience to those in authority, he urged his slaves to accept Christian teachings and coaxed them to attend services. Some were receptive. The Old Testament espe-cially appealed to many who heard echoes of their experience as slaves. Others were less than responsive, contemptuous of the tendency of some preachers to use the Bible to justify slavery, or just feeling that they had better ways to spend their precious time off than listening to a white preacher tell them what they should and should not do.

As the years went by, the home of John and Elizabeth Weaver be-came the linchpin of the community. It was a large, comfortable house, but seemingly never large enough for his rapidly expanding family. After Jacob, in short order Elizabeth bore him a daughter, Susannah, later to be known as Sookie, followed, at a rate of about one every two years, by Christiana, James, Mary, Kate, Elizabeth, Jack, Matilda, Christopher (or Chrisly as he liked to be called), and finally Montraville. So, over the years John expanded the house and made additional furniture by hand as it was needed: beds, tables and chairs, chests for holding the sheets, pillow cases, and "log cabin" quilts that Elizabeth, and then their daughters, made, cupboards for the baskets and foodstuffs, and a trough for the water from the spring,

John and Elizabeth also made themselves useful to the other settlers. John's blacksmith and carpentry skills were much in demand and highly appreciated. He was often called on to help with a variety of things his neighbor farmers needed. This was also a way he could repay the Cherokee for their hospitality, and perhaps convince them that they should not attempt to abscond, even if temporarily, with his children.

3

"Civilizing"

The Cherokee had no concept of "private property," although they did have tribal or communal lands which they regarded as essential for their needs, whether physical (farming and hunting) or spiritual. This resulted in conflicts with the settlers, some of whom were unable to understand the age-old customs and traditions of the Cherokee, who had been in America from time immemorial and in all likelihood had once hunted mastodons.

When John Weaver arrived, the Cherokee had a deeply-rooted community with a town council house atop a large mound. There, clan members would gather periodically to make decisions and meet with traders and officials. A constantly-burning sacred flame, made from seven different woods for the seven different clans, provided the source of the fires in the hearths of the dwellings surrounding the mound.

A "civilization program" was underway, instituted by government agents and preachers, encouraging the American "Indians" to become like the white man, in other words good Christian Americans. It seemingly enjoyed some success, but in fact there had been a great deal of "civilizing" going on simply due to the observation of and interaction with the settlers.

Whether or not all of this might be regarded as progress is debatable. (For one thing it should be borne in mind that among the practices learned by the Cherokee was the practice of slavery.) But, for better or worse, the Cherokee were in the process of setting up a rudimentary government structure. And many were abandoning their huts for log cabins and, in the case of the tribal leaders, even frame houses. In addition, gender roles were shifting.

Cherokee society had always been matrilineal, with descent traced through the mothers and homes centered on the wife's clan rather than the husband's. And Cherokee women at all times played a pivotal role in their communities. But in the past the women had worked primarily in the fields and the men in the hunting grounds. Then, as hunting became less prevalent (and less necessary), Cherokee men became responsible for the cultivation of crops and the raising of livestock and poultry. They were able to focus their energies on increasing crop yields and improving their homes.

So the women left the fields and, with housing becoming more "civilized" and complex, more and more took on the role of home manager. They looked after the young, cooked, made clothing and weaved baskets, and tanned hides, and so forth. But in addition they essentially governed the property, and the goods and chattels. In fact, it could be said that while the men built the homes, the women not only ran and controlled them, but owned them.

Elizabeth marveled at this, and especially at the fact that Cherokee wives seemed, for all intents and purposes, to be the heads of their households. When a decision needed to be made about homes or household property, they made them, and they even seemed to have the final word over the (male) leaders of their clans.

With the area becoming more and more populated with settlers and their rapidly growing families, and the government favoring the settlers and land speculators, disputes were inevitable. Many settlers, especially those who had little or no interaction with the Cherokee, had a low opinion of the Indians. As an example, the North Carolina legislature, in a report to Congress in 1827, stated:

[T]he red men are not within the pale of civilization; they are not under the restraints of morality, nor the influence of religion; and they are always disagreeable and dangerous neighbors to a civilized people. The proximity of these red men to our white population subjects the latter to depredations and annoyance, and is a source of perpetual and mutual irritation.

On the other hand, relationships in the Rims Creek valley and on the Dry Ridge remained for the most part harmonious. Goods were exchanged, information and requests were passed on, the two "tribes" got along. Montraville and his brothers even enjoyed watching Cherokee stickball games, and as they got older tried to play in them, but neither their parents nor the Cherokee would permit this. There was a reason why the game was called *a ne jo di*, "the little brother of war."

The goals, two tall poles, were hundreds of yards apart and the teams needed to score twelve times to win. There was much whooping and shouting, body contact at speed, and wrestling. The rules were vague and the action was non-stop for upwards of two hours. It was incredibly violent; broken bones were inevitable. The Weaver boys and their friends had to content themselves with less violent pastimes, such as the "chunkey game," in which a stone disc was rolled along the ground, and then spears were thrown in an attempt to strike as close to the disc as possible.

Montraville was especially adept at this game. When he played with his older brothers, he would almost always win, so often in fact that they eventually decided they no longer had any use for it. So Montraville's only real competitors were the Cherokee, who marveled at his skill. One young brave, the son of Chief Bowl, struck up a friendship with the youngest Weaver. His name was Chea Sequah, Red Bird, and he was as proficient at the chunkey game as Montraville.

On the sly, the pair would also practice using the ball sticks. Montraville wanted to be ready should his father ever permit him to play in one of the Cherokees' games. He became so accomplished, even better than Red Bird, that the boy offered to give him his sticks, saying that the best player deserved to have the finest there were. And indeed, Red Bird's sticks were the finest, made from the best, the most-supple hickory, which the Cherokee referred to as "sacred wood." The wood had been chopped and carved, thoroughly dried, and then steam-heated and curved back to form a small paddle-sized frame, with a pocket webbing of squirrel hide.

But Montraville knew that he would never be allowed to play in a game. The Indians wouldn't like it, and his father would forbid it. So he reluctantly continued using sticks he borrowed from one of Red Bird's brothers who had been badly injured in a game and no longer had any desire to play.

In any event, the lads had plenty of ways to amuse themselves. With other children, both Cherokee and settlers, they would play hide 'n seek and a version of tag called pickadill for hours at a time, and then roam the area, fishing in the creek or climbing Hamburg Mountain. The boys would tell each other, as they began to learn each other's languages, tales of their ancestors. Red Bird heard about John's exploits in the War of Independence and his journey with Elizabeth and Jacob to Rims Creek, while young Montraville learned about how Red Bird's father and the Cherokee people were being constantly pressured to give up land they considered their own.

Red Bird related how the Chief often talked about the likelihood that the Cherokee would be forced to move westward, as some, mostly young braves, had already done, drifting away like birds from the nest. Montraville's father had told his son that when he arrived in the area there was a community with dozens of families. But many had since de-

camped to the large colony near the Tennessee border, along the Oconaluftee River. Others had decided that they had no future anywhere
near the white man and had set out for the Arkansas Territory, nearly
1000 miles away, across the Mississippi River.

One fine day in early spring, the children were at their secret fishing
hole, attempting to land some brown trout, Red Bird with a bow and
arrow, Montraville with a fish-gig his father had made for him. As often
happened, the conversation came around to their narratives of the past.
Young Weaver was astonished to hear that the Cherokee had fought on
the side of the British in the War of Independence. "Doesn't that mean
that you are my enemy?"

Red Bird replied: "In our clan, the elders tell tales of our chiefs traveling to the great city of London in England many, many years ago, long
before the war. There they received the promise of the English king that
he would protect us from the people that had come from England who
wanted to take over our land. So the English were our friends. We could
not turn against them in war. Besides, why would we want to support the
Americans, who made treaties and then violated them before the ink was
dry, settling on lands that have been ours as long as the stars have been in
the heavens?

"Those people who want to take our land are all around us. There
are many who do not want to live alongside us and desire to push us out.
Here, in this place, now, we are friends, we get along fine, the Cherokee
and most of the Americans. But that can change. Enemies one day can
be friends the next, and friends can also become enemies. My father says
that he wants to be friends with all the settlers, and live in peace with
them. But he knows that the two people are different, and have customs
and goals that are in conflict."

"You and I are not so different," said Montraville. "I think of you as
a brother, and nothing can change that." He would never forget his

friend's reply: "I too think of you as a brother, but there will come a day when that will change."

In the meantime, for the most part, disputes between the settlers and the Indians were resolved amicably, albeit warily. The Chief had been among the signers of the treaty of Holston in 1791, through which the Cherokee accepted the "protection" of the United States and boundaries were established between the young country and Cherokee lands. In addition, via the treaty, US citizens could not settle or hunt on Cherokee lands. But as one might expect, boundaries were not fixed, and settler encroachment continued.

John Weaver was careful to avoid obtaining any landholding that the Cherokee might regard as something over which they should have sovereignty. And as one of the settlers able to communicate best with the Cherokee, John was often called upon as a conciliator. One day, a newly arrived settler trying to put food on his family's table had brought down a deer. While examining his prize, he was surprised by two Cherokee braves who disarmed him and allowed him to run off, sans deer. He had been hunting on what the Cherokee considered their territory. John, recognizing that the man was simply unacquainted with the customs along Rims Creek, offered to negotiate.

"Chief, this man did not know that he should not be hunting on that land. He was only trying to provide food for his family. He has now learned what he can and cannot do, where he can hunt and where he must not. Please return his rifle and I assure you there will be no further problems with him." So said John Weaver, using English he thought the Cherokee would understand mixed with the Cherokee language which he had obtained.

Answered Chief Bowl: "John, I cannot do that. There must be some punishment for this stupid man, and you know that under the Treaty I have the authority to administer that punishment, which will be the loss of the weapon he used in an attempt to steal food from my people."

"Duwali, I know you like chicken – I promise that I will deliver to your village five roasted chickens in return for the man's rifle. That will more than atone for his actions."

After taking a moment to consider the matter, and perhaps thinking about how tasty those birds, prepared by Elizabeth, would be, the Chief replied: "John, I know that you are a good man, and I will accept your trade. This time. Because this situation is becoming worse. Not a moon passes in which one of your people does such a shameful thing, or even worse, settles on our lands.

"And when I object, some government official shoves some document, which I cannot even read, under my nose and says that I must 'compromise.' But tell me John, why is it that we are the ones who must always 'compromise?' The day is approaching when your people will take our lands and we will have no option but to find lands in the West."

And so, a few years later, it came to pass. The Chief led many of his people west in search of lands on which they could hunt and put down roots without the interference of white settlers. His son, perhaps more at ease with the white man's ways, stayed. But then, as we shall see, there came a time, when John was no longer around, and Montraville led the Weaver family, when the remaining Indians were forced to leave.

4

"Praise the Lord"

For John Weaver, nearly as important as establishing himself and his family at Rims Creek was the need to honor God, in thanks for his good fortune in finding such a promising land. He followed the Commandments to the letter. While he would work from sunup to sundown six days a week, he would not allow even the washing of dishes on the Lord's Day. John was a Presbyterian and one of the first elders of the Presbyterian Church along the creek. He and his slaves helped erect a magnificent house of worship, constructed of logs, which included a Negro gallery from which the seated black men and women could see and hear the preacher without catching so much as a glimpse of the whites below.

But a few years later, Bishop Francis Asbury, circuit riding for the Holston Methodist Conference, came along. John and Jacob were greatly impressed by the bishop. Who would not be? This elderly man was willing to suffer the discomforts and brave the dangers, from renegade warriors and wild animals, of constant travel in the wilderness to bring the gospel to people who might never have the opportunity to sit inside a church.

Asbury, considered the founder of American Methodism, and called by some the "George Washington of American Christianity," traveled tens of thousands of miles, preaching countless sermons throughout the Colonies and, after the War of Independence, the United States. In 1771, at his home in England, he had felt the call of God and had left his family for the New World, unsure if he could find the words that would move people to the Lord, but convinced that he must try. When the war began, he was the only Methodist minister in the Colonies. His message appealed to the courageous men and women who endured endless hardships and led a constantly precarious life on the frontier:

> Lord, we are in thy hands and in thy work. Thou knowest what is best of us and for thy work; whether plenty or poverty. The hearts of all men are in thy hands. If it is best for us and for thy church that we should be cramped and straitened, let the people's hands and hearts be closed: If it is better for us; for the church, — and more to thy glory that we should abound in the comforts of life; do thou dispose the hearts of those we serve to give accordingly: and may we learn to be content whether we abound, or suffer need.

When the bishop preached in a courthouse that had been built by Colonel David Vance and other settlers, in what was then called Moriston or Morristown, John and even young Jacob were much taken with the message and the messenger. So inspired was John that he carved out a lot from his property on the south end of the Dry Ridge to build a meeting place. The entire community worked on cutting logs and hauling rocks for the chimney, and in 1805 the First Methodist Church of Rims Creek was open to all comers.

Elizabeth, John, and Jacob were thus among the first members of the new church and by 1810 they were helping to organize local camp meetings. These had originated as simply a way for the far-flung settlers to occasionally get together, for a few days to a week, for fellowship and games, or just to get reacquainted. But the circuit riders realized an opportunity when they saw it. The camp meetings soon took on a religious tone — the Second Great Awakening come to Appalachia — and became revival services, "quickenings," that reinvigorated people's souls and encouraged sinners to repent. Attendees found plenty of food, family camping, praying, preaching, hymn-singing, and an all-around good time.

There was a county fair-like atmosphere in the gathering together of folks from as far away as 30 miles, arriving on horseback or wagon, often with a cow tied at the back to provide milk for the duration of the meeting. People would pitch tents and set themselves up for what many, if not most, considered the highlight of the year.

This was not your sedate church service – the attendees did not call themselves "shouting Methodists" for nothing. Cries of "Praise the Lord," "Hallelujah," "Glory, Glory, Glory" and "Amen" interrupted the preachers. The meetings often became frenzied, with shrieking, shaking, shuddering, and above all, singing.

Then there was the exhorting. Only the preachers could preach, but anyone could exhort, and many did, with spirited testimonies of conversion, or homilies and soliloquies of the believers' experiences in the faith. Family prayers and public prayers and preaching occurred from eight in the morning until the dying of the light in the evening.

Eventually, cloth tents and brush arbors gave way to log houses and cottages. The facility attracted the best ministers from far and wide. There were weddings and baptisms and, of course, conversions. And it would go on and on, from the first trumpet call at daybreak on the first day, getting everyone up and ready for prayer, until the last preacher, days later, called for a closing hymn and walked through the grounds shaking hands with all within reach.

John and Jacob helped build the rudimentary facilities — camping areas, platforms, plain slab seats for the attendees and the rostrum with its bench long enough to accommodate several preachers — and were prime movers in preparing the grounds every year. They made certain that the tent areas were swept and raked, the benches were scrubbed, and, in general, the place was made clean from top to bottom. At the same time, Elizabeth and the other wives would be baking up a storm, breaking out the preserves, and preparing huge quantities of bean dumplings and other victuals for their families.

But the best part of the festivities for the Weaver family came when, with great pride, John was able to entertain Bishop Asbury, near the end of the bishop's life, in the Weaver homestead, a short ride from the camp ground. To the amazement of John and his family, the bishop, though in poor health, regaled them with stories, speaking with considerable self-deprecation of his circuit-riding days, which he modestly described as "an opportunity to meet and pray with a handful of Christians, a great many hypocrites, and more than a few backsliders."

And that is how Montraville made his acquaintance, impressing the bishop with a demonstration of his knowledge of the Bible. When Bishop Asbury asked the seven-year-old Montraville what he had learned from the Holy Book, the lad recited by heart from Matthew 22:

Thou shalt love the Lord thy God with all thy heart and with all thy soul and with all thy mind. This is the first and great commandment. And the second is like unto it: Thou shalt love thy neighbor as thyself.

The elderly bishop was so impressed he called the boy to him and embraced him, saying: "You are going to be a wise and virtuous man," as tears streamed down his face.

Eventually, the prominence of the Reems Creek Camp Ground (somewhere along the line folks must have decided that "Reems" was more pleasing to the ear than "Rims") grew to such an extent that the 13th session of the Methodist Holston Conference was held there in 1836. This was the first such session in North Carolina, and the Weavers and other families pitched in to erect a Conference House at the camp ground.

35

It was, indeed, a beautiful spot, with age-old oak trees, grassy knolls, and crystal clear streams. In 1844, Montraville and another preacher, his brother-in-law Andrew Pickens, deeded to the church an additional five acre plot of land for a new Conference House for another Holston Conference at what was now called the Salem Camp Ground.

This was to be the last Conference before the schism over the issue of slave ownership by Methodist clergy resulted in a northern and southern Methodist Episcopal Church. The official Church position had always been antislavery, but it was never enforced. However, the Church leaders were feeling increasing pressure from the northern membership and clergy to take a stand.

The break was precipitated by the suspension of a bishop, James Osgood Andrew, who owned two slaves. The southerners disputed the authority of the Conference to discipline bishops. And there were also simple but significant cultural differences between the northern and southern Churches. While many in the southern Methodist clergy were unsympathetic to slavery, others saw "broad-mindedness" on the issue as a way of attracting well-to-do slave owners. This attitude perhaps made the split inevitable. But it had little impact on Montraville and the rest of the Weavers, who accepted slavery, that most "peculiar institution," as the way of the world.

5

"A Thirst for Knowledge"

Montraville grew up fast. He had to, what with so many siblings vying for attention. Nowadays, we might be concerned that he was a candidate for "youngest child syndrome." But while there was plenty of love and care from his parents and siblings, there was no coddling, and there was always plenty to do. And John and Elizabeth made sure that all their children had a role in the efficient running of the household.

Montraville did not have to be prodded by his parents. He loved anything to do with animals. He could spend hours grooming the horses, feeding the hogs, milking the cows. There was no formal schooling, maybe the odd session in the log church or other field schools, but John and Elizabeth, who had long before learned her letters with her husband's help, quickly realized that their youngest had a thirst for knowledge which they needed to foster.

There were no blackboards or slates, no grammars or arithmetic books, but John had fashioned a crude hornbook with the letters and numbers, and another with the Lord's Prayer. Elizabeth, often at night, after a hard day's work, if she were not too exhausted, would huddle with her youngest child, bent over the hornbook, and later the Bible and an almanac.

While his older brother Chrisly tired of Bible lessons, usually soon after they had begun, Montraville could never get enough. And even though there were times when he seemed frustrated with the limitations of his "education," he could often be found sitting by himself, studying the family Bible or doing sums, which his father had introduced to him when he was but four years old.

Elizabeth loved reading to him books by her favorite author, William Hamilton Maxwell. She was especially fond of his *Border Tales*, legends of the Scottish Highlands. And in short order Montraville became an even more capable reader than she was and offered to read to her!

Some books were available for purchase in Asheville. They had found their way from Charleston or Richmond to itinerant peddlers or to the Baird brothers' store. Bedent and Zebulon Baird had arrived in the area a few years after John Weaver, famously carrying a wagon of goods over the Saluda Mountains. The pair had become the first merchants in the community.

One of the books they sold was the aforementioned *Charlotte Temple*, which Montraville came upon one day in a cabinet he was not supposed to be looking in. But it is safe to say that he enjoyed far more the books about his hero, Daniel Boone, including John Filson's *Life and Adventures of Colonel Daniel Boon* and Daniel Bryan's *The Mountain Muse*, containing a 5,600 line epic poem about Boone. And he gobbled up the works of Sir Walter Scott and James Fenimore Cooper.

Unlike Chrisly and, it must be said, most of his other brothers and sisters, with the notable exception of Jacob, Montraville took a keen interest in religion, anxious whenever Sunday came around to get off to the Methodist church. He also couldn't get enough of the camp meetings, and he never had to be reminded to say his bedtime prayers, even making up his own. This pleased his father no end and he would seek to encourage Montraville's interest in any way he could. And eventually it paid off for both of them. The youngest Weaver was ordained as a Methodist preacher in 1829, the same year that, on December 30, he married Jane Eliza Baird.

Jane, two years Montraville's junior, was of Scots ancestry. Her great-great-grandfather had settled in New Jersey in 1683. Her father was the prosperous merchant Bedent Baird.

A few years earlier, Bedent had set up a household with his wife Jane Welch Baird in Beaverdam, a few miles from the Weavers. In addition to running his store, Baird bought and sold land, and had established the first grist mill in the area, delighting Montraville's mother (and father) no end since it meant easier-to-make and better-tasting bean dumplings. So the Weavers invited the Bairds to the Salem camp meetings and, while Bedent was not of an especially religious nature, the families got on well. And Montraville and Jane hit it off immediately.

She was intelligent, with a sharp wit, an easy laugh, a gorgeous singing voice, and a down-to-earth nature. And although two years younger than Montraville, she had in fact had more exposure to the world outside Reems Creek than her beau, having attended for a time Newton Academy School in Asheville, riding on horseback the five or so miles from her Beaverdam home to the school first established in 1793 as Union Hill.

The courtship lasted only a couple of weeks, if that. One Sunday they were chatting after church and the following Sunday they met before the service and attended together. It was generally held at the time that when a young man was observed walking a young woman to and from church they were officially courting. So what came next surprised no one.

Montraville had seen "love knots," woven from wheat, with ears of grain symbolizing fertility hanging from the knot, and he knew they had become popular with young men in wooing their sweethearts. And he thought about asking his mother, who was skilled in the art of wheat weaving, to make one for him. But he was too embarrassed to admit what he was about to do, and what if Jane turned him down? So he carved a "love spoon" in secret.

In truth, it was not much of a carving, little more than a cross and heart above the bowl of the spoon, and a bit rough. Perhaps the lack of quality was due to his nervousness or his having to work in secret, since he was a highly skilled woodworker. In addition to the furniture he made for the family, he loved to make toys, such as gee-haw whimmy diddles and spinning tops for his nieces and nephews. But, as they say, it is the thought that counts. And then of course Montraville had nothing to worry about. Getting Jane alone, which was no easy task given the slew of relatives accompanying both of them, he gave her the spoon.

Jane, giddy with joy, immediately accepted the spoon and his proposal of marriage. That night he broke the news to his family, who were thrilled (especially Elizabeth, who loved collecting grandchildren). Then there was only one more hurdle, the formidable Bedent Baird.

The next day Montraville rode over to Beaverdam and asked young Jane's father for her hand. Mr. Baird expressed some concern about the swiftness of the courtship. Montraville assured him that his parents were in favor of the match, as of course was Jane, but Bedent would not grant the request straight away. Still, after talking it over with Jane's mother, and of course Jane herself, he agreed to ride over to the Weaver place and give them the good news.

The wedding was held in the Methodist church. The custom at the time was to have the ceremony at the home of either the bride's or groom's parents. But John and Montraville especially wanted to hold the ceremony in the church. It seemed more practical given the number of people that were likely to attend, and they felt the best way to sanctify the union was to hold it in the House of God.

As was customary, Jane's big brother Elijah rode over to fetch Montraville. "Well aren't you the fancy man," said Elijah, eyeing the groom's dress coat, complete with vest and new fly-front trousers, and even a top hat. "I've only ever seen you in buckskin, but then I suppose you don't get hitched every day."

"Maybe so, but at any rate, for Jane, nothing but the best."

"In that case, we had better be gettin' on. I have been told that I must get you to the church on time or I'll have to answer to my sister, which I have no interest in doing."

"How is she? Can't be as nervous as I am!"

"Not nervous at all. She even said her cat sneezed when she was at her toilette this morning, which apparently promises a happy marriage. Personally, I think it was caused by the perfume she was puttin' on and spreadin' around. I was sneezing too!"

"Can't say I much like that cat, but perhaps now I should reconsider! Let's go!"

The church was packed and all was in readiness. Jane had a new dress for the occasion: a light blue serge apron-front affair with a plain bodice closed at the front. And her smile lit up the room. The service was short and sweet. In no time at all the preacher had pronounced them "man and wife" and they had leapt over a broom, officially signifying that they had jumped from life as single persons to a married couple.

There was quite a turnout for the reception in the home of John and Elizabeth. And who were all these people? It appeared that Chrisly had invited a few friends, and they were hoping for a good time, lubricated by some home brew.

But that was not to be, given the Weaver family's devotion to temperance. (Montraville was later to address the Flat Creek Temperance Society on the evils of intemperance to persons, the society, and the community, recommending that individuals "touch not, taste not, handle not the unclean thing.") Consequently, all the attendees got was the mildest punch, and a piece of the enormous dried apple stack cake, to which at least a dozen relations and friends had donated a layer, making it reputedly the tallest cake anyone could recall seeing.

There was an element which obviously could not resist sampling some liquor that had been introduced surreptitiously. These folks (and, yes Chrisly Weaver was at the forefront) seemed eager to get an early start to the new year celebrations. So they began an impromptu shivaree, banging pots and pans, hootin' and hollerin' until the couple came out and consented to a largely ceremonial ride around the house, Montraville on a rail and Jane in a washtub. The elders, and the fast-approaching night, put a perhaps premature stop to the merriment. None too soon as far as the couple was concerned. They had only one interest, getting into bed, which they did. And some nine months later, their daughter Mary Ann came into the world. But that's another story.

If ever there was a marriage made in heaven, this was it. Jane and Montraville found they were eager sexual partners, able to please their mate as well as themselves. But they also reveled in the loftier concerns of the soul, discussing the Bible, consulting Adam Clarke's commentaries and, as Jane had been exposed to more worldly literature, sometimes reading other books aloud to each other (although Montraville steered Jane away from *Charlotte Temple*).

One cousin reputedly had the largest library in western North Carolina, more than 500 volumes, with books ranging from a biography of Benjamin Franklin to Thomas Paine's *Rights of Man*, and from *Don Quixote* to Walter Scott's *The Lady of the Lake*. Another, Mira Margaret Baird Vance, the daughter of Bedent Baird's brother, Zebulon, was a passionate reader of books by the likes of Tacitus, Pope, Milton, and Shakespeare. She loved nothing better than reading aloud to her children, everything from *Pilgrim's Progress* to *Ivanhoe*.

Jane taught Montraville how to play the dulcimer and, although he wasn't especially proficient at it, eventually they were able to make beautiful music together, outside of as well as within the bedroom.

Since all of Montraville's brothers and sisters were now married, had moved out of the main house, and set themselves up on their own, and since John was now 66 years old and feeling his age, Montraville would be managing the farm. So Jane became a committed, full-time member of the John Weaver family.

She was an able and willing apprentice to the magic of Elizabeth's cooking skills and never shirked her household duties, usually rising before dawn to make sure everything was in order. She supervised all meals and took over much of the gardening work that had become too difficult and tiring for her aging mother-in-law, and found that she had a green thumb. Her garden produced food crops in abundance as well as flowers that brightened the house inside and out. Jane became adept at weaving and hand sewing, knitting and spinning. She made and mended clothes for the entire family. All skills that she, in turn, would pass on to her daughters.

Meanwhile, Montraville went from strength to strength on the farm. The cattle he and his father raised were the best for miles around. His skills as a blacksmith and brick maker brought folks from far and wide to seek his help. He involved himself in all aspects of the farm and was never hesitant to pitch in when another hand was needed. His slaves generally worked from sunrise to sunset, but so did he. In fact, everyone on the estate was expected to do as much in a day as his or her physical condition would permit.

It was perhaps this intense work ethic that caused some who did not know him well to find him a hard man. And a hard man to know. But those who encountered Montraville when he was performing his ministerial duties saw a very different side. Those who thought him perhaps less than affable in his farming duties may have been surprised to encounter this warm, compassionate, cheerful preacher.

In the pulpit he eschewed fire and brimstone, lacking the thunderous delivery that characterized many of his more celebrated compeers. But his passion for the Lord was unmistakable. He knew his Scripture cold and was able to speak on any Bible topic extemporaneously.

It must be admitted, however, that there were those who found his preaching a bit too oratorical. Perhaps it was his tendency to intersperse his sermons with lessons from his favorite authors, including of course

Sir Walter Scott. Some were a bit puzzled, for instance, when he spoke on the subject of adversity: "We are like the herb which flourisheth most when trampled upon."

In any event, he always kept in mind his congregants' real problems and concerns and was able to relate them to the Bible (and *Ivanhoe*), often discovering answers which people found helpful. He had a particular aptitude for home visiting and counseling and never turned down a request for assistance, sometimes riding several miles in miserable weather to comfort the sick and dying.

Jane would never forget the time when the son of a farmer who lived near Sandy Mush Creek came by in a driving rainstorm. The farmer had a deserved reputation as a stern, uncompromising man who treated his wife callously and his slaves brutally. He had had ugly quarrels with Montraville when he had attempted to get involved. The son was convinced that his father was breathing his last and demanded that Montraville go see him. In spite of the fact that the trip would require a long journey with a ferry across the French Broad, Montraville readily agreed.

"Are you sure this is a good idea? He is likely to throw you out as soon as you step through the door," suggested Jane.

Montraville replied: "I have never seen eye-to-eye with him. But that doesn't change the fact that I have a duty to perform, and I must do it."

When, many hours later Montraville returned, he told Jane that when he arrived the man was already dead. "But it was not a wasted trip. I was able to comfort the children and his wife, who despite the cruelties that had been heaped upon her was distraught at the man's death. And perhaps most important, my conscience is clear, and I have done what I was put on this earth to do."

6

"In Decline"

John knew he would not last much longer. He put on a brave front, but sometimes he could hardly catch his breath after the least exertion. He had coughing fits for no good reason. It seemed like every part of his body took turns becoming sore and inflamed. The girls kept up a steady supply of patent medicines, vile tasting stuff, to no good effect. Elizabeth tried all sorts of home remedies, none of which provided any lasting benefit: stewed beans as a poultice, slippery-elm tea, ashes in cider, lamp oil on a lump of sugar. Letty, the new midwife, attempted to weave her magic with various herbs and potions, also completely without success.

Chief Bowl sent a medicine elder to have a look at John. The elder prescribed a strong tea from the dandelion, to reduce inflammation, hemlock, to improve his breathing, and an infusion from the leaves of blackberry, which was supposed to stimulate his entire system. When they didn't work, he set fire to mullein roots and had John inhale the smoke.

Eventually he concluded, or so he said, that John's body was in decline and that there were things he could do to make him more comfortable, but there was no way to stop the natural process that was underway. John agreed. He couldn't farm, he couldn't ride, he couldn't hunt, he couldn't enjoy eating. He could pray, which he did of course. And he enjoyed listening to Elizabeth and Jane read to him. But in truth, what was the point of hanging on?

He had not been feeling well at the wedding, and had had to absent himself from the reception earlier than he would have liked. Now he had one goal: to see the birth of Montraville's first child. With that in mind, it was necessary that he set his affairs in order. His sons were, to his mind, well-settled, and each with a stable trade or profession. The same was true for his daughters, all now married and with their own houses and families. Montraville alone had no house, and he must remain with the farm to take care of Elizabeth. She was still in good health and John thought her likely to outlive him by decades, but she was beginning to show her age and could not run the farm by herself.

"Son, I'm not going to last forever. Now don't say anything, you know I don't have much time left. Don't deny it. You've seen what has become of me. I need to make everything nice and legal, so we must go to the courthouse."

Montraville looked over at his father, sitting up in his bed, where he spent most of his time these days. The light streaming through a window to the south lit up the room and this perhaps made his father look even more haggard than he had appeared in recent days. His sparse gray hair was disheveled, his face clearly evidenced the discomfort he was in, and his breathing was labored.

"Father, I know you must have a will. I've been thinking about it. And I know you want me to take care of Mama, and you know I will, whatever you decide. But are you able to make the trip today?"

When John had arrived in the area 43 years before, there was no Moriston or Morristown, let alone Asheville, and of course no courthouse. In fact there was no Buncombe County. It did not come into existence until, named for Colonel Edward Buncombe, a hero of the War of Independence, it was carved out of Burke and Rutherford counties in 1791. John Weaver had been one of the settlers who signed the petition to the General Assembly holding that there were "a sufficient number of inhabitants to form a respectable County."

"I am feeling well enough for one last journey to town. And it must be done. You will take over the farm. I want there to be no question about

46

that. You're the best of the lot, I know I shouldn't say it, but 'tis true. Let's say no more. Please ready the carriage."

Back then, in spite of recent improvements, the way into Asheville was difficult. Although the Buncombe Turnpike, a new route from the Tennessee line to the South Carolina line, had recently been completed, there was as yet no easy way to access it from Reems Creek by wagon. And the direct route into town was rutted, narrow, and twisty. If anyone in another wagon was encountered traveling in the opposite direction, there were obvious complications, since turnouts were infrequent. In addition, recent rains had left the track muddy and tricky to maneuver. Still, Montraville, after making his father as comfortable as possible, was able to make good time on the journey, pulling up to the new brick courthouse, which had been erected east of the public square, shortly before noon.

"Father, you stay here for a bit. I'll go in and see what we have to do to make the arrangements."

Montraville tried to adjust his father's blanket, tucking it in. But John was having none of it. "Son, I'd greatly prefer to come in and get this over with as quickly as possible. Help me down."

So father and son entered the courthouse, Montraville going in search of the clerk while his father set himself down on a bench in the corridor. Soon Montraville returned with John Woodfin, the clerk of court.

"Mont tells me you are desirous of finalizing your will. We can certainly do that but it might have to wait until after lunch. It will be easier to round up the necessary witnesses then."

"Thanks John, we've brought along a basket that Elizabeth put together. If it is all right we will just sit here for a spell and eat up the contents."

This they proceeded to do, although it must be said that neither man had much of an appetite. Perhaps the journey, or the task at hand, had seen to that. But, after a bit, men started ambling into the courthouse and it wasn't long before Woodfin was back, having collared three men who he said were willing to witness the signing of the will.

"John, or Mont, it is not necessary for you to pronounce the will out loud, but for the benefit of the witnesses, Seth Alexander, John Chambers, and G M Daniel, all Asheville residents, it might be for the best."

"If it is acceptable, I will do so for my father," said Montraville. "Here goes:"

I, John Weaver, being of sound mind & memory. My will is that should I decease first that my property be keep as is now under the care controll of my son Montraville Weaver for the maintenance of my wife Elizabeth during her life. At her decease, I give to my son Montraville Weaver the land whereon I now live, containing 672 acres with all that belongs to it for ever. I give unto my six dtrs. Susannah, Christina, Mary, Elizabeth, Matilda and Catharine all my household furniture to be equally divided at their mother's discretion. I give the balance of my personal property of negroes, stock, farming tools, still and such like to my sons & dtrs. Jacob, James, John & Christopher G. Weaver, Susannah McCarson, Christina Vance, Mary Addington, Catharine Pickens, Elizabeth Wills and Matilda Garretson at the death of their mother, Montraville having his share in the land. I ordain my sons Jacob & John Weaver as executors. Signed, John X Weaver.

At the conclusion of the reading, Woodfin asked: "John Weaver, is that your last will and testament?"

John replied, "Yes it is."

"In that case Mr. Alexander, Mr. Chambers, and Mr. Daniel, please sign at the bottom as witnesses to this document."

On the return journey, a somber mood overtook father and son. There was little conversation. But eventually John said: "That's done, Mont. Now I can rest easy, in my mind at any rate. And my body will rest soon. I do not see how I can continue this way. But as God is my witness, or perhaps I should say 'God willing,' no reason to risk bringing down His wrath on me, I will see your child into this world."

And for a time John seemed to improve. Was it the sheer relief of having the will over and done with? Was he just putting on an act? More likely it was due to the fact that Jane was spending as much time as possible with her father-in-law. In fact, it was while she was sitting next to him, reading to him from *The Last of the Mohicans* (yes, Montraville's passion for Fenimore Cooper had spread), that she first experienced an intense contraction. There had been mild cramping for a couple of weeks and she had felt the baby move lower in her abdomen the previous week, accompanied by an increasingly achy lower back. But this was decidedly different. It was a pain she had never felt before.

"Jane, what is it? Are you all right? You're in pain aren't you?"

"Yes father, oh my, I think this may be the start. We had best fetch Letty."

Jane had not long before received some sage advice concerning child birthing, during a visit to her cousin Mira, a couple of days before Mrs. Vance went into labor with Zebulon, her third child, who would grow up to be a Congressman, Confederate Army officer, Governor, and Senator. Mira was an admirable woman, looked up to by everyone she met, universally regarded as cheerful and witty, more than capable of running the farm when her husband was away on his frequent business trips, and as comfortable in society as any lady from Asheville. She and Jane had instantly bonded over their shared love of books.

While the pair had been drinking blueberry herbal tea in the kitchen of the Vance home in the Reems Creek valley, Mrs. Vance opined: "I would not say that birthing a child is the easiest thing in the world, but it is not anything to be frightened of. Yes, there is pain, but it is bearable. I've gone through it twice before and have survived just fine. The first time I did feel like I was getting punched in the stomach, but that only lasted for a little while, then there was just truly bad cramping. There's lots of pressure and you will be exhausted through and through. But it is so worth it!"

"That is reassuring, Mira. But when you had Laura, you were much older than I am. Does that make a difference?"

"My midwife told me that the older the mother the better, which did give me a bit of confidence. But I've since found out that that is an old wives' tale!"

At any rate, when the time came John was much more nervous than Jane, who was in raptures that the baby might actually be on the way. It had not been a terribly difficult pregnancy, but that did not mean that she wanted it to continue. Frankly, she was tired of the coddling she had received, including the many hours spent with Letty, who, at Montraville's direction, sat with her in case there was anything Jane might want. She well knew that there would be more than discomfort ahead, but she wanted it over with.

Jane was, to be sure, more than grateful to Letty. She was not a proponent of the "fussing" that many midwives favored, including beautifying the mother-to-be by such things as braiding her hair, and greasing and powdering and perfuming her body. But she had started a massage regimen that made Jane relax and probably eased her discomfort. In addition, Letty was able to sneak Jane a swig or two of the medicinal spirits that the midwife kept hidden away from John and Montraville.

Letty was not just a midwife, as she was happy to tell all and sundry. Her skills at healing and birthing had been passed down from her mother Hannah, who had brought most of John and Elizabeth's children into the world. But she had gone to meet her Maker a couple of years earlier after a run-in with an ornery bull. Letty was young, somewhere in her mid-twenties, and had had a hard time establishing herself as a healer after the death of her mother. But when she nursed Elizabeth through a bout of influenza several months earlier, her standing had been secured.

At this point in time, a midwife was about the only option. The area's first physician, Dr. Robert Brank Vance, Mira's brother-in-law, had attended the Weaver family on a couple of occasions. However, he had been shot above the right hip by a political rival three years earlier in a duel, dying a day later. (He reputedly threw away his shot.) So Letty it had to be.

When John, suddenly as nervous and excited as an expectant grandfather should be, called out for Elizabeth, she appeared so quickly that she must have been aware of what had been going on and dropped whatever she was doing. "You had better find Letty. I think she is needed."

But Letty too was close at hand. Something had told her that she should not stray far. As she entered the room she practically yelled: "Missy, is you in pain?" But one glance at Jane provided her with the answer. "We need to git you up to bed."

By this time Montraville too had arrived, panting and ashen-faced. "What can I do?" he blurted out.

Letty replied smartly: "You can leave this room right now and go back to doin' whatever you was doin'. And don't even think about goin' to the birthin' room until I says so. It is no place for any man. There is nothin' to worry about – we are jest goin' to let nature take its course." But then when he turned to go, after giving Jane a hug and a kiss on her cheek, Letty had one more request: "Wait now, give me your hat. This will go real smooth if the missus can wear your hat."

Montraville was momentarily dumbfounded, but was quickly put in the picture by Elizabeth: "I always wore John's hat during labor. It seemed to lessen the pains."

Soon, Jane was lying in the birthing room, with Letty in constant attention, comforting Jane with her words and her hands. Montraville and John were seated in the kitchen, anxiously awaiting the birth. And late that evening, Montraville, crying tears of great joy, was able to place his daughter, Mary Ann Elizabeth Weaver, in her grandfather's arms.

And not two months later, John slipped quietly and painlessly away.

7

"Across the River"

The decade of the 1830s was one of happiness, comfort, and security for the Montraville Weaver family. Every other year a new child was welcomed into the household while the farm continued to prosper. Such was not the case for Red Bird and his family.

In 1830, Congress had passed the Indian Removal Act, which established Indian territories out west in exchange for the eastern tribes relinquishing their lands in the east. The Cherokee nation had naturally objected and even won a case before the Supreme Court. Despite this, President Andrew Jackson, refusing to enforce the court decision, continued to seek the relocation of all Cherokee from their lands in North Carolina and other nearby states to a territory west of the Mississippi River. However, Jackson took no overt steps to remove the Cherokee. Instead, a new treaty, which came to be called the Treaty of New Echota, was proposed, ceding the Cherokee lands east of the Mississippi in return for money and the new territory in the West.

This treaty divided the Cherokee nation. Many had already left, moving to the Indian Territory, what is now Arkansas and Oklahoma. Others felt that it was only a matter of time before they would have to move. For years there had been ever-increasing incursions on their lands, especially in those areas where gold had been discovered. Some also felt that the Cherokee were becoming too much like the white man, adopting his culture, his agricultural practices, his language, his religion, and even owning slaves. They felt that removal to a new land would counter those influences and make the Cherokee a true nation again.

Still, most Cherokee opposed removal. Snows had prevented those living in the Carolinas from attending the meeting at which the New Echota treaty was discussed and voted on. So the treaty was signed in 1835 by a minority group of unelected Cherokee, the so-called Treaty Party. It was then approved, in an altered form that greatly disadvantaged the Cherokee, by a margin of one vote in the United States Senate in 1836.

Even then, the Federal government took no action to forcibly remove the Cherokee until 1838, when President Martin Van Buren ordered the mobilization of Federal troops and General Winfield Scott requested massive numbers of volunteers to carry out the removal. And on May 10, 1838, Scott issued an ultimatum: His troops were ready. The Cherokee must voluntarily report to camps from which they would be relocated to the west or be hunted down and taken to the camps by force.

So Montraville was not surprised when, later that week, Red Bird came to his home, and he could easily tell from the expression on Red Bird's face that assistance was needed. And time was of the essence.

"I fear that I know why you are here. You need to move. How can we help?"

Red Bird and Montraville, like brothers in their youth, had grown apart as time went on. With the ever greater responsibilities each faced, and their growing families, it was no wonder that they would find little time and few chances to get together. But there was never any doubt in the mind of either of the men that if the need ever did arise for one to assist the other, that assistance would be forthcoming.

Red Bird explained: "You have no doubt heard that the military has asked for volunteers, including a regiment of men from Buncombe County, to remove us from our lands. And before you say it, I do know that no member of the Weaver family would participate in such an action. But, yes, we need more than that. We are going to slip away into the mountains, for we have no intention of going to the West. The mountains are our home. They can be harsh, but that is fine with us. The harsher the better – we believe that the government will not be interested in a handful of peaceful fugitives hidden away in a rugged, unforgiving wilderness."

"My good friend," said Montraville. "I still find it hard to imagine that this is happening, and that anyone thinks it necessary. We are not even in Cherokee territory and there are so few of you left. And I am certain that there is little sentiment in the county on behalf of your removal. If you don't mind my saying so, I think that most of my fellow citizens regard you as only slightly less white than they are."

"Maybe so, but it no longer matters, if it ever did. Remember, your President Washington asked us to 'become herdsmen and cultivators', which we did, forsaking our hunting traditions. Last year we harvested 180 bushels of corn per acre and none of it went to making whiskey.

"Your President Jefferson wanted us to adopt the structures of your republican system of government, establish written laws and courts, and take up private ownership of property, which we did, forsaking a way of governing that had worked well for generations.

"We now have an alphabet, a constitution much like your own, a newspaper. We teach our children English, and many of us have abandoned our former religious beliefs. No one any longer speaks of our traditional values of harmony and balance and reciprocity. We no longer look for the good in a person first; we now look for the evil. We now worship your God, who I must say has always struck me as vindictive and harsh. Not when I hear you preach. But it is what I hear from so many other sermonizers.

"In spite of all this 'civilizing,' your President Monroe saw the need for us to move west to make room for more and more settlers.

"And do you remember what your President Jackson, whose life and reputation were saved by our great Chief Junaluska at the Battle of

Horseshoe Bend, told him? 'As long as the sun shines and the grass grows there shall be friendship between us, and the feet of the Cherokee shall be toward the East.' Then a few years later he insisted that we could not live among you, could not be 'civilized,' and had to be sent hundreds of miles away, for our 'protection' from harassment by the white man.

"Countless promises and treaties over the years have been broken by your leaders. Now your President Van Buren has made it clear that he wants us out, by force."

"Red Bird, my friend, how many people are you talking about? And where will you go?"

"It is only my family. The rest of the clan has decided to remain. They are thinking with their hearts not their heads. They are even planting for the summer crop, a crop no Cherokee will be around to harvest. I have sold or given away much that we have. Whatever happens, the others will say nothing of what we have decided to do, and they will maintain our home as long as possible to conceal the fact that we have left. We will disappear into the mountains to the west until things settle down and we can be assured of a place where there is a future for us.

"I am hoping that you and one or two others who you are confident will say nothing about this will help us cross the Turnpike and the *Tahkeyostee*. Of course, I know these waters. But it will be difficult, especially with the children. I cannot manage it alone. Also, you can assist in case there is any difficulty with the authorities. Once we have crossed the river, you will return to your homes, and we will vanish.

"We should leave after dark and follow Reems Creek to the river. I believe we can arrive before dawn and prepare for a crossing at first light when there will be little chance of traffic on the Turnpike or the river."

"Since you are determined on this course," assured Montraville, "my family will do whatever is necessary to assist. I believe I will call on Chrisly to help, and Jack lives near the mouth of the creek so he should be able to provide information, and even cover if something goes wrong."

56

"Nothing must go wrong. Every day we remain here I become more and more fearful that we will not be able to escape."

Montraville felt that there was little danger of interference at that point from the Federal or State authorities, but if what Red Bird was saying were true, how long that situation might last was anyone's guess. So, one night the following week, aided by a full moon, the Cherokee set out for the French Broad, along with Montraville and Chrisly.

They were to meet up with Jack before first light, about a quarter mile north of the mouth of the creek. Chrisly, three years older than Montraville, and now a sober family man, was as dependable as the stars in their courses. Jack, on the other hand, was considered by many the black sheep of the family, living some way off and perhaps being a bit too fond of the gay life and apple brandy. But his brother was confident that he would pull his weight when the chips were down.

Traveling overland, hugging Reems Creek and avoiding the main roads and settlements, the party reached the Buncombe Turnpike. This route was heavily used in the fall and winter by drovers, with stands set up to cater to travelers. But at this time of the year it was mostly utilized by stagecoaches on regular schedules. They were able to cross the road without difficulty and, it was hoped, without being seen. Then there was only the French Broad to negotiate.

Jack had earlier found what he thought was the best spot for the crossing, with no habitations nearby and a reasonably shallow riverbed. But when they met up, he expressed some concerns. "The river is quite full, as full as I have seen it in recent days. Still, it is good that we are doing this so early. It might be impossible later in the day. Anyhow, it will not be easy. Montraville and Chrisly, we should have no problem, but I am worried about our companions."

Red Bird, more nervous than Montraville had ever seen him, replied with uncharacteristic sharpness: "So am I. That is why you are here!

If I were alone and we had more time I would love to race the rest of you to the other side."

The duly chastened Jack muttered an apology and then decided that it would be best to keep his mouth shut and defer the arrangements to Red Bird and Montraville.

The seven Cherokee: Red Bird and his wife, Ama, his mother, Nanyehi, and four children ranging in age from 6 to 16, had two riding horses and four pack horses carrying all their worldly goods. It was decided that the Weavers would assist Ama and the younger Cherokee in making the crossing on the Weavers' horses, while at the same time leading the pack horses.

Red Bird then took charge: "Dustu, you ride with me, and I will lead one of the pack horses. Nanyehi, you take Leotie. Ama, go with Chrisly, and Immokalee, you go with Jack. Mont, Oukonunaka is the youngest and the least mindful so he is your companion. I think we should all try to stay together and if anyone has a problem the nearest rider will assist. Remember, there are bound to be some deep pockets in the river, and there are large stones everywhere. So proceed with caution."

But the trek had hardly gotten underway before there was trouble. The pack horse being led by Red Bird balked when the water reached its flanks. The horse then tried to reverse direction, pulling Red Bird's horse, named Gola, Cherokee for winter, as he was white as snow, to the side and spilling Dustu into the water. Red Bird was able to reach down and just barely grasp his hand, pulling him back onto his horse. But this made it immediately clear that attempting to lead the pack horses across the river at the same time as Red Bird and his family attempted to cross might not be the best choice.

"I think we will have to change our plans," shouted Red Bird as he returned to the river bank.

Once the group had reassembled on dry land, he asked Montraville: "What do you think? I was hoping we could get across quickly, but I believe I placed too much confidence in the ability of the pack horses to deal with the river."

"Yes. The most urgent thing is to get you and your family across and out of sight. We will have to see if it is possible to walk across leading the pack horses. If you take Oukonunaka, and go with the others, I will stay here with the pack horses and Dustu, who I believe is tall enough and strong enough to cross on foot. When Chrisly and Jack return, the four of us will together walk the pack horses across."

"You are of course right," agreed Red Bird. "Get over here Oukonunaka. We will lead, then Nanyehi, Chrisly, and Jack."

With that, Gola, carrying Red Bird and his youngest child, gingerly reentered the river, with the others following. About twenty yards from the bank, with the water lapping the flanks of the horses, Nanyehi attempted to pass her son. But her horse stepped into a depression and she was violently thrown forward, with Leotie clinging on for dear life.

"What on earth do you think you are doing, *etsi*? You know that this river is dangerous. Do you want to lose your granddaughter," exclaimed Red Bird. Nanyehi replied with a shout and slap to her horse, which regained its footing and surged past.

Montraville, watching from the riverbank, could not stop himself from chuckling, in spite of his concern. He had always admired Nanyehi's fearlessness and resolve, and knew that Red Bird felt the same. Nanyehi had strongly objected to the decision of her husband, Duwali, to lead most of his clan to the new territory several years before, and had received her clan leader's permission to end the marriage.

In any event, after what seemed like an eternity, but which was in reality only a few minutes, the four horses (and all their riders) were across the river. The Cherokee melted into the forest, while Chrisly and Jack turned around and were headed back.

"The riverbed is quite uneven, and the current fairly strong," noted Chrisly on his arrival. "These pack horses are going to be a problem."

"I think this will work," said Montraville. "We can reassure them if they are alongside us instead of trailing us. And we can pick our route better that way. Are there any deep spots we should watch out for?"

"Sure, but nothing we cannot avoid. And on foot we can see where we are going. Besides, I'm due for a bath," Chrisly declared with a grin.

"Let's get the horses out of the open," urged Montraville. "We can leave Dustu here with the pack horses and be back in fifteen minutes. Jack, Lucinda can deal with the horses can't she?"

"Don't see why not. She wanted to come with us but I told her it would be better if she stayed at the house in case there was any trouble."

A half hour later, the threesome returned. Some time had been lost getting the horses settled and convincing Jack's wife, who felt she should join the men in case something went wrong, that she needed to stay put. But it was still early enough for them to be fairly well assured that no one would witness the goings on. They were mightily impressed to discover that Dustu, rummaging around in the trees, had found sticks that he was able to fashion into rudimentary poles for each of them. Montraville, grabbing one, exclaimed: "Excellent idea, why didn't we think of that?" and started for the water.

Each Weaver led a pack horse, and Montraville in addition made sure that Red Bird's elder son had no difficulties. "Dustu, keep hold of the reins of the horse and face upstream. And make sure you watch where you are planting your feet. The riverbed is uneven and rocky. Don't try to go straight across. Kind of angle yourself downstream. You will fight the current less that way. Oh, and roll up your pants legs. There will be less resistance to the water's flow that way."

With that, the foursome entered the river, a nervous Montraville leading the way. All seemed to be going well, with the horses apparently taking comfort in the close proximity of a person. But at about the mid-point of the river, Dustu stepped on the side of a rock and fell, pulling his pack horse down with him. The horse righted itself quickly, but Dustu was struggling to get back to his feet. Montraville grabbed him by his collar, making sure that his head remained above the water.

"Are you all right, Dustu? Can you walk?"

"I may have injured my foot," replied Dustu. "It hurts like the devil."

"I'm going to bend down. See if you can climb up on my back. And take the reins. Then I'll see if I can lift us both."

This he did, and with some difficulty Montraville and Dustu, with a horse on either side, continued crossing the river. Chrisly, ever the joker, could not resist shouting: "Quit playing around you fellows, this is no place for pick-a-back rides."

When they had finished the crossing, and Dustu had climbed down, a concerned Ama rushed to her son. He could not put any weight on the injured foot. "You will have to ride. But quickly, we must get away from here."

Red Bird, with what certainly looked like tears in his eyes, embraced Montraville and thanked him for everything, most importantly the rescue of Dustu. "My friend, I fear this is the last time we will see each other. I owe you so much and can never repay you."

Montraville replied: "That is not how I see it. Your friendship over so many years has no price. I owe you for that, and for the education you have provided me into the ways of your people and the land that we both love. If you ever need anything, you only have to ask and it will be granted. Now go!"

"I feel the same way," replied Red Bird. "As I think I explained to you once, a long, long time ago, there is no word in Cherokee that is equivalent to the English word 'please,' because when we Cherokee ask for help from another Cherokee, we know we will receive it. In many ways, you, to me, are another Cherokee. When I have needed anything, you have provided it. Now you have helped provide the means for us to continue being Cherokee in this, our land. And I know you will continue being a Cherokee, in spirit, when we are all gone from here.

"So, as a last token of my friendship and appreciation, when you return home you may find something to remember me by."

Then, Montraville heard a voice, close, and familiar, but at the same time seemingly far, far away: "Wake up Mont! I've been watching and listening to you for an hour. You've been twitching and mumbling up a storm. That must have been some dream."

"Oh my, Jane. You have no idea. I just helped Red Bird and his family cross the river. Isn't that crazy?"

"But you've been hearing all that talk about Indian removal, the call for volunteers, and didn't he once say that one day he and his family would be heading across the river?"

"Jane, yes, he did, and I do recall he said something like that. But I never took it seriously, and if I had I would naturally assume he meant by the ferry or James Smith's Bridge. There is no possibility of fording the French Broad River, leastwise anywhere in this vicinity. Where on earth did that notion enter my brain?"

"Maybe because he often spoke about the river being sacred, being purifying. And I remember you relating how you sometimes went with them when you were young, when his whole family would journey to the river for the going-to-water ceremony. And how you once, as a joke, tried to take part and were lifted out of the river by Red Bird's father and dumped on the bank."

"Yes, that is true. Maybe that's why I dreamt that he wanted to cross in the river, not over it. But at any rate, in the dream he asked for our assistance in leaving before they were expelled. Jack and Chrisly helped. It was so vivid! And terrifying at times. I need to go see Red Bird right now."

But after dressing hastily and gulping down a cup of coffee, what should he find when he opened the door but Red Bird's treasured ball sticks. And when he made the trek to Red Bird's cabin, he found no one. There was an unnerving emptiness, matching the emptiness in his heart. Not just Red Bird, but all of the Cherokee had taken flight.

Red Bird and his clan vanished into the hills, never to be heard from again. They may have been among the fortunate ones who were able to hide out, until the Army departed the area in November 1838, and eventually be welcomed across the Oconaluftee River in Qualla Town. Those who remained, including hundreds scattered throughout western North Carolina, "innocent and simple people into whose homes we are to obtrude ourselves," according to one of the Army officers, were brutally rounded up.

Soldiers surrounded their homes, kicked in the doors if there was any sign of resistance, and hauled away any Cherokee that could be found, without giving them an opportunity to pack their belongings. Many families were broken up, some women were raped, and their homes were looted and then burned to the ground. They were marched to Fort Butler, more than 100 miles distant, where they were housed in camps near the Fort.

But far worse was to come. After Fort Butler they had another long journey to the emigration depot, effectively a series of concentration camps, at Fort Cass in Tennessee, where thousands of Cherokee languished for months. The planned journey by steamboat utilizing the Tennessee River was made impossible by a severe drought that depressed water levels. Hundreds died in the camps from dysentery, exposure, dehydration, whooping cough and other maladies. Food was scarce and putrid, infested by weevils. There were no vegetables; there was no milk. So, many died of starvation and food poisoning. Then, just as winter was setting in, they were forced to set out for the designated Indian Territory.

None of the Cherokee who were displaced had an easy time of it, but those who had been evicted from North Carolina and the others assembled at Fort Cass had it the worst. There was tremendous suffering. The winter was one of the coldest ever recorded. There was snow storm after snow storm. Streams froze solid. The Mississippi could not be crossed for weeks because of ice floes, resulting in an extended stay along its still-swampy banks, miserable for the troops, deadly for the Cherokee. There was little medical assistance and grossly inadequate shelter. Food was even worse than in the camps; good food was nonexistent. Everyone was vulnerable to the elements and weakened by disease, hunger, and exhaustion. Thousands died.

When the "lucky" remainder finally arrived in Oklahoma, they found terrain that bore no resemblance to their traditional lands back east. Food promised by the government was not provided. And there were tensions between those who in effect had agreed to the relocation, the Treaty Party, and those who had opposed it. Violence, including assassination, was rampant.

As to whatever happened to Red Bird and the others who left with him, nothing is known. The Army arrived shortly after they left and, finding no one there, had simply set fire to whatever remained.

8

"That Dark Beverage of Hell"

"I must say I was a doubter when the Temperance Convention recommended that our societies meet on Christmas Day, but this turnout certainly justifies that advice. There are many folks I have never seen before at a meeting, and probably more than this old log church has ever seen. But the proof of the pudding will be when we see how many take the pledge."

This was Reverend John Siler Weaver, Jacob's son, standing next to his uncle Montraville at the back of the church, as they surveyed the crowd of some 90 people who had gathered for the quarterly meeting of the Flat Creek Temperance Society, of which Montraville was an Executive Committee member.

Montraville too was impressed: "I even see a couple of people that have been notorious troublemakers in the recent past, due I would certainly think to their intemperate ways. Wonder how they were dragged here. I suspect that Reverend Morgan and his son had to do a lot of convincing."

From the time of John Wesley the preachings of the Methodist Church had always been strongly tied to temperance. Wesley himself abhorred alcohol and sermonized: "You see the wine when it sparkles in the cup, and are going to drink of it. I tell you there is poison in it! and, therefore, beg you to throw it away." So, unsurprisingly, a large part of the mission of the traveling Methodist clergy (including, for eight long years, John Siler Weaver) involved attempts to induce their preachees to abstain from "ardent spirits."

When John, the elder, and Jacob Weaver had been persuaded by Bishop Asbury and the other circuit riders to take up Methodism, they also subscribed to temperance. Asbury even railed against "fiddling and drinking," casting a pall over the traditional evening dances, which he felt were just an invitation to binge on alcohol. Montraville's father, in his Presbyterian days, had had two copper stills for brandy-making, but the bishop's eloquence persuaded him to dismantle them and quit the business entirely. And when, at his death, the remains of the stills passed to his children, Montraville and James cut the tops off and the big pots were thereafter used for boiling clothes and cooking up apple jam and peach butter.

Buncombe County, like much of western North Carolina, was beset by moonshiners and even had a couple of fairly sophisticated distillers. All the farmers grew corn, which loved the cool mountain climate. But it was difficult to market. A mule could carry at best something like four bushels of corn, but could haul the equivalent of 24 bushels of the much more profitable liquid made from the corn.

And drinking was certainly widespread. The average early 19th century American drank seven gallons of liquor per year, and without doubt the average western North Carolinian exceeded that amount. Liquor was common at meals and social events, and virtually universal among those who had not found religion. Many feared "milk sickness," a debilitating disease caused by ingesting the milk from cows that had eaten snakeroot, a poisonous herb. They and others were persuaded by the view that spirits were actually healthful and nutritious, in other words "good for what ails you." Mothers were even known to give a teaspoonful of diluted liquor to their colicky babies.

In 1831, the North Carolina Temperance Society was formed to combat the evils of "demon rum" and its effects. When, a few years later, the temperance movement took hold in Buncombe County, Reverend

John S. Weaver and Reverend Montraville Weaver were among the first to sign on.

"Mont, do you know what pledge they are going to use today? I mean, I've seen the new pledge the English have adopted and I must confess that it is finer and clearer than the one we've been using. Let's see if I have it here. Yes, here it is, see? The Teetotal Pledge: 'I do voluntarily promise that I will abstain from ale, porter, wine, ardent spirits and all intoxicating liquors, and will not give nor offer them to others, except as medicines or in a religious ordinance.'"

"I am assuming that last part is a nod to communion wine. Oh, if only we could find a way to get unfermented wine! Still, I would much prefer that we leave out any religious exemption. Why call attention to communion wine? As for me, the more direct and succinct the pledge, the better. There is nothing wrong with: 'I do hereby solemnly bind myself to abstain from all intoxicating drinks except when prescribed by a physician in case of sickness, and to further promise to discourage the use of them by others, in all laudable ways.'"

"But then what about communion wine?"

"Communion wine is not an 'intoxicating drink.' And no one is going to become an alcoholist, or relapse, from a sip of Holy Communion wine. Besides, if the prospect of a sip of wine lures someone into church, that is fine with me."

"With moonshine so easy to come by, something tells me that is not likely to happen. Anyhow, what is on the agenda today?"

"We need to appoint a committee to deal with this business of treating voters. We have these laws prohibiting candidates for election from providing voters with, shall we say, incentives. But the sheriff does nothing to enforce them and the situation has gotten out of control. The practice is not only a blight on our democracy but a major incitement to drunkenness before, during, and after voting day. At the last election the liquor flowed non-stop at every stand, inn, and tavern in the county, and people were passing out in the streets.

"We also need to select a committee of vigilance which will be a core group charged with acquiring more members and in general promoting the cause. I'm hoping you will be one of those members."

"I think I had better talk that over with Mary!"

"Come on now John, this is important. But then again maybe she would like to join also. I'd love to see as many women as men on the committee. After all, more women have taken the pledge than men and there are a goodly number who come to the meetings. They should be taking on more responsibility."

"Mont, you know as well as I do that they are happy to come to these meetings with their husbands, or perhaps better said drag their husbands to these meetings. But they are far too busy with running the house and taking care of the young'uns to get heavily involved. Plus more to the point their husbands won't let them."

"Well, we must try. This issue is of the utmost importance for families. So we will discuss the issue and see who is interested in volunteering."

"Or see who you can shame into volunteering."

"John, please. I am confident nothing of the sort will be necessary. At any rate, there is also going to be testimony about his struggles with demon rum by a man who farms over by Turkey Creek, then I'll say a few words, and then everyone (I hope) will take the pledge."

After the meeting was called to order, John intoned a prayer: "As we gather here in the shelter of God, we thank Thee for the blessings You have bestowed on our communities and ask that You strengthen us, restore us, and inspire us with Your love so that we may carry out the work set before us, take our promises to all the earth, and save the souls of those who have not yet found the way of the Lord. Amen."

This was followed by a spirited rendition of the Temperance Doxology:

Praise God from whom all blessings flow,
Praise Him who heals the drunkard's woe,
Praise Him who leads the temperance host,
Praise Father, Son and Holy Ghost.

Then the committees were filled, or it should be said almost filled. As Montraville remarked to John: "There seems to be a certain lack of commitment with regard to these committees," to which John, no doubt trying to reconcile his own reluctance, chose not to reply.

Next, Mr. Willie Biggs was called on to testify, but again there seemed to be a great deal of reluctance. The woman next to him, presumably his wife, appeared to be urging him to get up, or was she pushing him away? At any rate, in time, Mr. Biggs was able to get to his feet and start to speak, or perhaps it would be more accurate to say start to mumble.

"He seems a bit unsteady, Mont. And do I detect a flask stuffed down the side of his boot?" asked John, who, glancing to his right, saw his uncle with his head in his hands.

"Hidee, ever'one. Hope y'all will scuse airy problem I might could have up here, but I'se jest about as nervous as a cow with a buck-toothed calf.

"Mah name is Willie. I'se 52 year old and I gotta say, lucky to've made it this fur. If'n it weren't for mah wife, who must be 'round here somewhars, I'd not have made it this fur."

After scanning the crowd, possibly trying to spot the lady in question, he seemed to frown, and then continued: "I used to lak a drank or two, ... or more!" With that, the speaker chuckled and seemed to reach toward his boot, in the process stumbling a bit.

"Mont, it does appear that Mr. Biggs is a bit wobbly. I am not sure this is going to work out."

But the speaker righted himself and continued, now appearing to be on the verge of tears. "Anyhoo, mah wife, who's settin' rat ovair, I

69

b'lieve, spoke to me and spoke to me, boy cain't she tawk! .... anyhoo, she were right convincin'....so I took up with the Lord Jesus." And then, practically shouting: "I'se a new creation created in Christ Jesus for good thangs. Bad thangs has passed away, praise God!"

Now he was actually crying, and swaying on his feet. "Mont, do you think we should ease him out of here?"

"I don't rightly see how we can, John. We have to give him a chance," responded Montraville, now trying to suppress a grin.

The speaker continued: "So y'all can see, that ole drunkard is done done. Well, mos'ly anyhoo. But sometimes I jest needs a little halp. Lak now."

And with that, he did reach down to his boot and pull out a flask. A collective gasp rose up from his audience as he took a sip and continued: "Lak I said, sometime I jest needs a little halp. I started drinkin' when I were 13 year old. Why? 'Cause ever'one else were and beside, it made me feel so good. I drank 'cause I wanted to. And I got hooked. But I has seen the light! I'se hooked no more, no more, no more...."

As his attention seemed to drift away, a couple of people did likewise, making stealthily for the door. And everyone else in the audience was whispering to each other. Montraville felt that it was now time to take action.

"Thank you Mr. Biggs for that moving testimony. Now I think we should proceed to the rest of the agenda." But Mr. Biggs was not through.

"I ain't done done Rev Weaver. As I were sayin', I means as I were about to say... Now what were I goin' to say? Oh yep — I fought the battle of the bottle fer many a yar. Thar were times when I were drunk as a skunk an' I'd cry out for halp. I wanted to stop drinkin', but the desire fer the bottle were stronger than I were. Booze had me; it were in control. But now I'se licked it, or jest about anyhoo. I ain't had nary a drink for yars before this here meetin', well, leastwise weeks, ... or a couple a days...."

"Or a couple of minutes," whispered John to his uncle.

Now Mr. Biggs was giggling and again reaching for his boot. But all of a sudden he seemed to realize that he had his flask in his other hand and he overcorrected, causing him to stumble and virtually fall into the neighboring woman's lap.

Montraville, again trying to keep a straight face, said to the woman: "Ma'am, I think this may have been a bit too exciting for Mr. Biggs and it is probably a good idea if you helped him back home."

"Reverend Weaver, I'm sorry but I never saw this man before to-night. I'm certainly not his wife! I think the man has mistaken me for her."

If Montraville was taken aback by this turn of events, he hid it well. "Ladies and gentlemen, does anyone know Mr. Biggs and can help him on his way?"

Not getting any takers, he suggested to the hapless speaker that he rest a bit, and moved to the front of the meeting house to address the fidgety crowd, many of whom were now clearly in the process of departing.

"Ladies and Gentlemen, let us reflect on what we have seen and heard tonight. Mr. Biggs is not an evil man, nor even a bad man. I know he is a good man, who has had the misfortune to be captured by demon rum, that dark beverage of Hell. He is a perfect illustration of why our work to remove the greatest hindrance to the acceptance of the Gospel is so extraordinarily important. And we must not turn our backs on those who, like Mr. Biggs, have taken the wrong path. It is essential that we work ceaselessly to reform, through kindness, not through condemnation, each and every drunkard.

"It is a good work, an important work, important to our families, to our Church, to our society, to our great state and nation, and to the world. There are those, even God-fearing, abstaining men, who believe that this work is unworthy of the attention of lofty minds. Nothing could be further from the truth. No one can doubt that ardent spirits are at variance with Divine Law, that ardent spirits corrupt the body, that ardent spirits cripple the intellect, that ardent spirits injure the soul, that ardent spirits disrupt family life, that ardent spirits are a horrendous waste of time and money.

"We must continue this struggle with the Devil, yes, with the Devil. Every day, more and more people are being sucked deeper and deeper into this Satanic whirlpool. We must oppose with all our might the production, the vending, the imbibing of these demonic brews. To that end, all who believe in this glorious cause should enlist by signing the pledge being put forward tonight."

And with that, one by one those God-fearing folks, the few that were left at any rate, came to the front of the meeting house and signed the pledge.

"So.... that went well!" noted Montraville as he and John locked up the church. "Maybe a Christmas meeting wasn't such a good idea after all."

To which John, himself now grinning, could only reply: "Amen to that!"

9

"The Only Socially
Responsible Thing"

There was a fair amount of abolitionist and manumission sentiment in the Piedmont of North Carolina in the first half of the 19th century, leading up to the War Between the States. The Quaker community around Greensborough was in the forefront, producing the likes of Levi Coffin, often called the "Chief Engineer of the Underground Railway," Daniel Worth, convicted and sentenced to prison for "circulating incendiary material against slavery," and William Swaim, abolitionist editor of the *Greensborough Patriot*. Then there was Hinton Rowan Helper of Mocksville.

Helper, a tall, well-built man who always wore a spotless, full broadcloth suit, wrote *The Impending Crisis of the South: How To Meet It*, which severely attacked slavery, arguing that it harmed the economy of the South and was an impediment to growth. The book was taken up by the Republican Party and widely distributed in connection with the presidential campaign of Abraham Lincoln. It is now regarded, next to *Uncle Tom's Cabin*, as having had the greatest literary impact on the road to secession and war: "Proslavery men are working for the disunion of the States, and for the good of nothing except themselves."

A popular bonfire item throughout the South, the book and "Helperism" are credited with stoking the fires of secession among the political leaders spearheading that crusade. They saw it as an attempt to divide Southerners along class lines. While they might acknowledge, in private, that slavery really only benefitted the planter class, they would nonetheless argue that it was necessary for the Southern economy, and they feared that white non-slaveholders would turn against them if they came to believe that there was an "impending crisis" caused by the slave economy.

In any event, there was not much anti-slavery sentiment or activity in the western North Carolina mountain country. It appears that no one from the mountains, and certainly no one from Buncombe County, joined the North Carolina Manumission Society, which promoted the voluntary freeing of slaves by their "owners," an activity made extremely difficult and dangerous through roadblocks thrown up by the state legislature. Nor were there any local affiliates of the Society for the Colonization of Free People of Color of America. This group, founded by Henry Clay and other prominent politicians, and supported for a long period by Abraham Lincoln, sought to assist freeborn Negroes and emancipated slaves who were willing to settle in Africa.

But the slaveholders of that time and place knew little of Mr. Clay and nothing of Mr. Lincoln, who at the time was just an obscure politician given to radical views such as:

If A can prove, however conclusively, that he may, of right, enslave B why may not B snatch the same argument, and prove equally, that he may enslave A? You say A is white, and B is black. It is color then, the lighter having the right to enslave the darker? Take care. By this rule, you are to be a slave to the first man you meet with a fairer skin than your own.

You do not mean color exactly? You mean whites are intellectually the superiors of the blacks and, therefore, have the right to enslave them? Take care again. By this rule you are to be slave to the first man you meet with an intellect superior to your own.

But say you, it is a question of interest; and if you can make it your interest, you have the right to enslave another. Very well. And if he can make it his interest, he has the right to enslave you.

At any rate, nobody in his right mind gave any credence to anything of the sort in western North Carolina, and while there was plenty of Unionist sentiment, and the slaves would have been, in general, better off than those in the cotton fields, the area was as wedded to the system of slavery as was the plantation belt.

Buncombe County had established slave patrols as early as 1794 and the county's slave population had been growing ever since, and was laboring in every economic sector: from livestock to hospitality and from mining to construction, and slaves were used as servants in the finest homes. Slaves also earned good profits for their owners by being hired out for road construction, including on the Buncombe Turnpike.

So it is understandable why Asheville's citizens might have been nervous about abolition and abolitionists, and so met at the county courthouse and adopted a resolution that called for local officials to start closely examining the actions and business of visitors to the town.

Having reason to believe that this portion of the country, like many other portions of the slaveholding states, is infested with itinerant Abolitionists, who under various disguises are endeavoring to sow the seeds of dissatisfaction among our slave population...be it resolved that all strangers, particularly those from non-slaveholding states who come in our midst claiming to be in pursuit of peaceful occupation, shall be subject to the most rigid scrutiny, and if there is probable cause to believe they are abolitionist emissaries they shall be taken up and made to undergo a searching examination and be dealt with accordingly.

Montraville Weaver and his kinsmen certainly knew of abolitionists, but it is likely they never encountered one. However, they did encounter the kind of "dissatisfaction" those troublemakers were fomenting.

Montraville at the time held ten slaves. Like most of his fellow slaveholders he was convinced, or at any rate had convinced himself, that freedom and the nature of the black man or woman were incompatible. He had heard about what the conditions were like back in Africa and, after all, if they could fend for themselves, why had so many ended up here, as slaves? Anarchy and penury would be the inevitable result if they were cut loose.

Accordingly, the only socially responsible thing for a white man to do, if he possessed a business or a home, was to govern the black men and women and protect them and organize their lives. To Montraville Weaver they weren't quite his children, and he did not exactly regard them as part of his family, but sometimes the lines got a little blurry. At any rate, he believed that his slaves were happy to have him in charge of their lives and felt they were appreciative of what he did for them. They certainly seemed cheerful enough at any rate.

For the most part, Montraville was pleased with his slaves. They worked hard. Usually six days a week, from dawn to dusk (as, in point of fact, did Montraville), with a couple of hours off for a mid-morning breakfast and an afternoon dinner. When there was field work to be done, all hands would be expected to snatch a hoecake or two and be ready to work at first light. Sure, there were surly looks and the dodging of work and sloppiness that all slaveholders liked to complain of. One was never sure if an illness claimed by a slave was real or an excuse for a couple of days off. And what could have become of those implements that suddenly seemed to have disappeared?

There was, naturally, petty thievery – the sort that went on routinely on any estate or plantation. Food, of course, and tools or, in the case of house slaves, cutlery. Montraville never could understand the need for thievery since he felt that his slaves were well-provided-for, with plenty of food (mostly corn bread or hominy, salt pork, beans and molasses) and what he regarded as ample clothing. Following his father's example, slaves were allowed a small garden for themselves to supplement their diet or even earn a little money from selling the sweet potatoes, beans, peas, peppers, and greens they were able to grow. And they were permitted to raise a few roosters and hens. So he turned a blind eye when his slaves helped themselves to animal feed to nourish the fowl they raised.

Montraville was aware of a secondary economy in which slaves would sometimes sell or barter goods, including, occasionally, stolen goods, with free men and other slaves on neighboring farms or in town. It was a fact of life. And as long as it didn't get out of hand, there was no point in interfering with it.

On Sundays and holidays (there was a break for Christmas of course and extra time off following Easter and Pentecost), his slaves were free to fish in the nearby creek or hunt for rabbit or other small game. New garments, or new cast-offs, were provided every year. The men received a wool jacket, a pair of wool breeches, a pair of linen breeches, a couple of coarse linen shirts, one or two pairs of stockings, and a pair of shoes, as well as a blanket. Women received a wool skirt and a couple of linen shifts along with the jacket, stockings, shoes and blanket. Women working in the house also received a simple dress, likely a hand-me-down, along with an apron and cap.

In addition, there were occasional surprises, including small amounts of cash or gifts, such as household items or additional clothing, for jobs well-done or for the performance of extra work. And there might be simple toys, such as a ball or a few marbles, for any young children. At any rate, Montraville was firmly of the belief that you will catch more flies with honey than with vinegar. So his old hickory stick got only occasional and limited use.

Punishments or, as he thought of them, corrections were more likely to consist of confinement to quarters, assignment to more onerous tasks, or additional work. Of course, the ultimate punishment, selling a slave to a cotton plantation in the deeper South, was always available if needed.

The slave quarters were typical, which meant barely adequate, but certainly better than in his father's day. Montraville suspected that too many people occupying a small space was an invitation to the spread of all manner of diseases, so the cabins were not crowded and provided something akin to privacy. The women occupied one of the frame, whitewashed "dog-trot" cabins, basically two large rooms with a breezeway in between, and the men occupied another, with a single cabin set aside for families. Each slave had a rope bed with a straw mattress.

The quarters were cold in the winter and hot in the summer, and dark and smoky virtually all the time. Rats, mice and all manner of vermin were ubiquitous and managed to evade even the rapacious attentions of cats and black snakes. Cleanliness may have been next to godliness, but in slave quarters it was also next to impossible. However, there were now raised wooden floors, better shingling, a brick chimney, and casement windows, so light and ventilation were somewhat improved. And Montraville made it known that if his slaves needed anything, within reason, that would improve their conditions, he was open to considering it. As long as they carried out their assigned tasks.

George was a six-footer with dark skin and hair to match. He was fit as could be, obedient without being servile, taciturn (a quality that Montraville especially valued), and with a manner that demanded respect from his fellow Negroes as well as the Weavers. He had been a neighbor's field slave five years before but had become available when the neighbor, who employed a white overseer and recognized George's capabilities, asked Montraville if he might be interested in using him as a foreman. He did not come cheap, but it was a transaction that Montraville had never regretted.

Now George was effectively the estate's overseer. He was given a free hand to deal with the other slaves, including the right to determine when they might need time off and rest on occasion. On the other hand, he never seemed to need time off, always appearing tireless and willing to pitch in and get his hands dirty when an extra body was needed to plow, sow, and harvest crops or deal with the estate's animals. If he had a fault, it was his love of the accoutrements that came with his position. Montraville was happy to provide him with fine boots and a whip, but if he ever used either to discipline the other slaves Montraville was not aware of it.

Jennie was a tall, slim beauty who was pursued unsuccessfully by every black man, free or slave, whose acquaintance she made. A few years before, on a plantation to the east, she had been the mate of a hot-headed drunkard who got himself killed when he made the mistake of taking on the master of that plantation. She was the house slave, helping Jane with the cooking, doing the cleaning, washing, mending and so forth, seeing to the fires, airing the bedding. She wasn't as submissive as many a master and mistress might like; she knew what she could get away with. But she did as she was told and did it well, including helping out in the fields when necessary, and Jane enjoyed having her around. And though it was not something Montraville wanted bandied about, when things were quiet, Jane was teaching Jennie to read and write.

Letty, approaching middle-age and increasingly it must be said on the plump side, also worked in the house, but she mostly looked after Montraville and Jane's younger children. Given the mischief they liked to engage in, this was for all intents and purposes a full-time job. But she did help out with the cooking and cleaning, especially when guests were expected, which was fairly often. And, while there now were medical professionals in Asheville, her healing skills were still called upon when any slave or family member was feeling poorly.

There was one family. Charlie, short, around 5 feet 6 with an easy manner, and Sally, a slim, long-limbed charmer, worked in the fields. Their two children, Ned and Julia, being only 10 and 12 respectively, helped around the farm, Ned running errands and gathering firewood and water, and Julia weeding the garden and helping to keep the slave quarters clean. Soon of course they too would be in the fields.

Montraville liked having a family among his slaves. Since slaves, as property, could not enter into a contract, they could not be legally married. But slave marriages were recognized by the participants and most masters, and Montraville was no exception. He was more than happy to respect them and, further, celebrate them, with some official-sounding language and Bible verses. He knew that most slaves lived with the same spouse until death, and that most slave children grew up in two-parent households. If, that is, they were fortunate enough not to be forcibly separated. And he figured that a black man who loved his family was less likely to cause trouble.

Montraville was confident about the loyalty of those slaves. This was less the case with a pair of young women, Bett and Sukey, whom he had inherited upon the death of his mother, and who worked in the fields and helped look after the livestock. Bett was pretty, flirty, and vivacious. So far she had not caused him much concern. On the other hand, Sukey, light-skinned, with long, straight, flowing hair, and relentlessly sullen, was known to have had relations with Cato, one of his brother James' field hands, and James had warned Montraville to be on the lookout for trouble. He felt they were capable of making a run for it someday.

James had also persuaded Montraville to purchase, for a token amount, Cato's friend Peter, believing that he would have more control over Cato if Peter were not around. And the latter had, so far, proved to be a diligent, obedient worker on Montraville's farm. But George was concerned that Peter had his eye on Bett. He had noticed the pair whispering to each other and discontinuing their conversation as soon as they saw that George was looking their way.

For almost a year the plan had worked. As far as the brothers knew, Sukey and Cato had seen each other only at church services, and even then they had not been allowed to converse. The brothers' properties were separated by nearly three miles, and slave patrols were active in the area. Still, neither brother imprisoned his slaves and it was always possible that they had been communicating through messages passed along by other slaves or, if they dared take a big chance, directly.

So it was not a complete surprise when George came to Montraville's bedroom, rousing him early on a frosty February morning, and said: "Massa, sumpin's up. Peter's sneakin' about in the stable and he have no bidness bein' there."

"Just him, George? Any sign of Bett?"

"I ain't seen her. Should I go check on her?"

"Maybe it is just Peter up to mischief. Stay with me while we see what's goin' on."

The pair headed to the front door and Montraville, opening the door a crack, thought he heard sounds like a horse and rider approaching from around back. Then, definitely, he heard whinnying coming from the direction of the stable.

"George, go fetch my Springfield, and wake up the missus if she is still sleeping."

Montraville quickly stuffed his feet into a pair of boots and opened the door wider, concentrating on the sounds he was hearing from over by the stable. Sure enough, there was activity over there. When George returned with Jane in his wake, Montraville said: "Jane, stay here. We're going to go see what the devil is happening. But keep the house dark."

What was happening, as Montraville, still in his nightclothes, and George soon discovered, was Cato astride a horse, with another horse in tow, and Peter in the process of leaving the stable leading two horses himself. Montraville was also able to glance over toward the quarters, some distance away, where Bett and Sukey should be sleeping, and thought he detected light coming faintly through a window.

As Peter mounted one of the horses, Cato, seeing Montraville with his rifle aimed at him, shouted: "Goddamn it Pete, we need to git outta here."

But Peter was already on the move, Cato following close behind. They may not have even heard Montraville yelling for them to stop as he fired his weapon over their heads, hoping they would comply without endangering themselves, or at least the horses.

But they were gone in a flash and Montraville was left standing there with his rifle as the miscreants continued on their way. He was tempted to immediately fetch a horse and go after them, but all he had on was a nightshirt and flannel drawers and he reasoned that the men would not be able to make much speed, especially with the two extra horses.

"George, go check on Bett and Sukey. Maybe those two villains were just trying to rustle those horses, but I'm thinkin' the extra mounts were for the girls. See if they are still here and if so stay with them. I'm afraid they might be planning on meeting up with that wretched pair down the road."

While Montraville ran back to the house for some warmer clothes, George did as he was instructed and discovered the two young women, all dressed up with, now, nowhere to go.

"I might've known," exclaimed George. "You is too stupid to live. The only ones dumber are those two young bucks you was plannin' on runnin' off with."

Naturally, the two pleaded innocence. They supposedly had no idea what was going on. "We don' know nuthin' — jest heard a racket and thunked we oughta git dressed."

Now lowering his voice, George calmly replied: "How dumb do you think I is, huh? You may not know it but dis is your lucky day. I has a kind heart and I'm goin' to risk mah neck to save you the beatin' you deserve. Now quick, git serious. You ain't goin' nowheres. I'se gonna help you out. Hide them bundles of your'n, git them clothes off and git back into bed. NOW!!"

At the house, Montraville told Jane what was happening as he understood it. "Go to the slave quarters. George is checking on Bett and Sukey. Let me know if they are still here, while I get dressed."

When Jane arrived at the slave quarters she found the young women scrambling into bed, with George surveying the scene. "George, what's goin' on?"

"Missus, they jest got up when they heard the ruckus and I'se told them to git back in bed."

Jane, however, could see that there was far more to the story. There was plenty of evidence that the girls had been planning to leave, including outer garments strewn about the cabin and a pair of bundles which appeared to have been hastily, but not effectively, hidden.

But, fortunately for the young women, Jane, while hardly an abolitionist, had never been able to disregard her disquiet with regard to the institution of slavery. Plus, she had a soft spot for Bett, who she had high hopes for, and she suspected that this episode had been orchestrated by Sukey and Cato.

"George, I am willing to overlook what is actually goin' on here. And I won't tell Mr. Weaver. But in case he decides to investigate the matter himself, get this place straightened up."

When she returned to the house she was able to report that "Bett and Sukey are still here, and under George's watch. Looks like they woke up when they heard something and were just curious."

"That's what George said? And you believe him? All right, have it your way. I don't have time to deal with them at the moment. Now I'm goin' to find Peter and Cato, and our horses, if I have to chase them to the ends of the earth. But first I'd better make sure James knows what is goin' on, and see if I can rouse some patrollers."

No sooner were the words out of his mouth than a rider came galloping into the yard shouting: "Am I too late?" James was livid with rage and seeing in Montraville's face what the answer to his question was he demanded: "Is Peter gone too? Any idea where they've run off to?"

"They can't have gone far. They hightailed it down the path beyond the stable, which you probably have figured out since you didn't encounter them. Each had a good mount and they were haulin' a couple of other horses behind them. If we can figure out where they were headed, we can get 'em."

"Were those nigger gals of yours with them?"

"They are still here. George says they weren't fixin' to go with Cato and Peter. Anyhow, if they were we stopped them before they could meet up with 'em. That's enough talk, let's find 'em!"

"Those nigger gals were goin' with them. Can there be any doubt? They must know where Cato and Peter are heading. Let's see if we can't convince them to talk."

"James, you know I wouldn't get any help from them. Even if they do know."

"You baby them, Mont, I've always said it. There are times you need to give these darkies a lesson."

"All right, what have you learned from yours?"

With that, James grimaced and through clenched teeth muttered: "Same as you, nothing."

"So what are we waitin' for. Let's find 'em. They haven't had much of a head start."

"Hang on a minute. Let's think. We know they didn't go toward the camp ground. I've just come from there and besides they wouldn't dare. And they wouldn't go towards Asheville. I'm betting they took the road up Hamburg Mountain, then over the top and down Flat Creek way."

"Makes sense to me James. Let's go."

But it was all for naught. After giving up the chase, without a sign of the two men or any of the horses, they had returned and roused a patroller who promised he would get some men together and be off as soon as they could.

Then the following morning a report came in that the bodies of two men and four horses had been found along the banks of the French Broad down toward Warm Springs.

"Jane, how could they be so stupid? Trying something like this in February! Attempting to cross the river with it half iced over! Dragging two horses with them! Which they didn't even need since they had no hope of joining up with Bett and Sukey."

"Yes, but I believe George. They probably took the extra horses just to finance their escape. Think what they could be sold for or used if something happened to the ones they were riding. As for why now, why try to cross the river, they were desperate, that's all."

"Why, Jane? I've always been good to them, to all my property. Is there a more tolerant master anywhere around these parts? You know everyone else thinks I'm way too lax with them. James, for one, was giving me hell for it."

"Dear, that may well be true but still they are human beings and yes, I know, our property. But do you remember that line from the Shakespeare play about the Jew I read to you awhile back? 'If you prick us, do we not bleed?' They are people, not like us yes I know but they breathe and feel and think. They have emotions and desires. Maybe they preferred a chance for freedom, no matter how slim, to being a slave. Maybe they just couldn't abide being anyone's property anymore."

10

"The Runaway Match"

A few years later Montraville found it necessary to visit the Reems Creek post office and decided to first stop by the new Vandiver general store. He didn't often bother with the newspaper but Jane had specifically requested that he check on something she had been hoping to see in it. Sure enough, there it was, right on the front page.

Montraville was so desperate to give the news to her that without a moment's hesitation he remounted his horse and headed for home, in spite of the fact that he had not attended to the business that had taken him to Main Street in the first place. But that could wait for another day. Jane had been on pins and needles wondering what had happened to the piece she had sent off to the editor of the *Asheville News* with much trepidation a few weeks before.

Arriving back, having made the journey in record time, Montraville burst through the front door shouting: "Janey, it is in the paper! On the front page!"

The voice that answered was no less excited: "Mont, I'm in the children's room, tendin' to Eliza Jane. Can you come in here?"

As Montraville placed the newspaper in her hands, he could see that she was smiling broadly through tears of joy. "There it is, right there on the front under Miscellany: 'The Runaway Match' by Jane Weaver."

"I can hardly believe it, Mont. And it looks as if they printed the whole thing."

"Well, as you know, I have not read it, since you refused to let me. But you can't stop me now!"

"Mont, I have a better idea. Why do we not gather together the children and I shall read it to everyone?"

Montraville hesitated briefly. He wasn't sure that was a good idea. It would mean a delay in his appreciation of his wife's literary talents and he had been itching to read the piece ever since Jane had told him she had submitted it. And what if it weren't any good? But, he reasoned, if that were the case, the paper wouldn't have printed it. So he reluctantly acceded to her request, and later that afternoon, Montraville, holding the baby, Eliza Jane, and surrounded by Maggie, Fulton, John, Will, Kittie, and Mary Ann, heard his wife read "The Runaway Match":

"Caroline, I wish you would remain a moment," said Mr. Warren, as his daughter was about to leave the parlor."

"Well, papa, what it is?"

She strove to look unconscious, but her varying color and the nervous movement of her lips betrayed secret agitation; in fact, she suspected the purpose of her parent.

"I thought," said Mr. Warren, "that when I forbade young Collins my house you were prepared to submit to the prudence of my decision. We talked the matter over, Caroline, if you remember, and I was at considerable pains to convince you that he was idle, wasteful and, I feared, dissipated—in short a very unfit person for any woman to trust her happiness with. You silently agreed to what I said—at least you said nothing in reply. I fancied I had persuaded you, for I thought your own good sense, to which I appealed, would see the matter in a light similar to that in which your mother and myself beheld it. Judge then of my inexpressible pain when I saw you walking arm in arm with him in the outskirts of the city today."

He paused, and Caroline hung down her head abashed. "I was not mistaken," she said to herself, "it was pa whom I saw."

Mr. Warren waited, for more than a minute for her reply, but as she continued silent, he went on.

"Now, Caroline," said he, "I wish you to look on me as what I am—the best friend you have in the world, and one who has no motive, much less any wish, to advise you wrong. It is a mistake of people, especially of those of your sex, to suppose that parents wish to tyrannize over them in the affair of marriage. Believe me, nothing is generally further from a parent's thought. It is not unfrequent, indeed, that a father differs from a daughter as to the wisdom of her mating herself with a certain suitor, but to such cases the father is nine times out of ten right, and the child wrong. The parent, from his knowledge of men, from what he hears in the street, and from other sources, usually arrives at a juster conclusion respecting a young man's character, than a daughter, who has little or no means of ascertaining the truth. In the case of this young man Collins, I know him to be extravagant, idle, occasionally intemperate in his habits, and head over ears in debt. Besides this, he has a violent temper. I beseech you, Caroline, do not give way further to this infatuation of yours."

As Mr. Warren spoke, he approached his daughter and took her hand. She burst into tears, looked up in his face and said —"Oh, but papa, I love him and he loves me; he says he will throw himself away if I do not marry him. Surely, surely I can, I ought to reform him."

Mr. Warren shook his head. "Caroline," he said severely, "this is sheer folly, miserable infatuation! No woman ever reformed a man whose principles were so loose as those of Collins; a wretch, who in his own words will throw himself away if you do not marry him. Listen to my words, child, for you are weaker than I thought, and I must rule where I would prefer to persuade: If ever you marry Collins, from that hour this house is closed against you."

The tears of Caroline flowed faster. Mr. Warren, after a turn or two across the room, softened again, and addressed her in kinder tones—

"My child," he said, "I speak thus for your own good; I know, if you marry Collins you will regret it; and I would, by interdicting it, spare you such future sorrow. I will not urge you to unite with any man you do not fancy, however excellent I think him to be. This I promise you; and on your part, I shall expect you to give up this acquaintance. Tomorrow I will look for your promise to this effect. Go now and think of it; I am sure you will obey me."

He stooped down and kissed her tenderly; and then Caroline, still weeping, rushed from the room.

But was it to think, as her father desired, of her duty?

Alone, in her chamber, she recalled, at alternate moments, the words of her parent, and the insidious persuasions of her lover; and alas! the latter had most influence with her.

Caroline was not exactly a weak girl, but she had fallen into a bad set at school, and derived from it many hurtful notions of a child's duties to its parents, especially in a case of supposed affection. She had read, not good novels, but visionary romances; and these had strengthened her mistaken ideas.

Her present suitor was a handsome libertine who knowing her father to be rich, desired to possess the daughter's hand, as with it went a large fortune.

The finished manners of Collins had easily won her liking — for we cannot call it love—and imagining herself to be in a similar situation to her favorite heroines, she regarded the opposition of her father as oppressive and unreasonable.

That very day her suitor had urged her to elope with him, and she had consented to do so. But her parent's kind expostulation had now for a time shook her purpose. Finally, however, the vanity of being the heroine of a runaway match, as well as her ill-based views respecting the supposed injustice of her father, induced her to fulfill her promise, and at the dead of night she left her home forever.

We say left her home, for she never had another. Mr. Warren proved true to his threat, and was the more inflexible because Caroline had eloped on the very night he had pleaded so earnestly with her. "She left me with my kiss still warm upon her cheek," he said; "she preferred another, and a stranger, to me; she treated me not like her best friend, but like an enemy, and henceforth she is banished from my heart."

Yes! she never again had a home. Her husband took her to a hotel, where they remained several weeks, hoping daily to receive a summons from her father; but as none came, they were forced at last to retire to a cheap boarding house. Here, amid indifferent society, Caroline, who had been tenderly nurtured, learned soon to feel acutely the advantages of which she had deprived herself, and learned to long for her old home.

If her husband had truly loved her, or if she could continue to persuade herself that her father had been unjust, she might have found some alleviation in her altered fortune. But her husband, angry that her father was inexorable, now began to punish Caroline for her father's firmness, by neglecting her and left her, evening after evening, to amuse herself, while he spent the hours at the billiard table, in the theatre, or with some gay friends over a bottle or two of wine. It was now that Caroline saw the correctness of the judgment which her father had expressed respecting

Collins. She not only learned that he was both idle and a spend-thrift, but discovered that he was intemperate, passionate, and unprincipled.

Often when he became excited by wine, he would address her in a most cruel manner, charging their present poverty on her, or rather on her "niggardly father," as he called Mr. Warren to her face. At last one night he returned in a violent state of excitement from the gaming table, where he had lost largely, and finding Caroline weeping had struck her a blow in a fit of passion that felled her to the floor, where she lay bleeding.

And this was the end of her dream of romance! Into this slavery, into this deep degradation had her vanity led here. Ashamed to tell the truth and throw herself on her father for protection, she endured for more than a year, every variety of in-sult from her husband; her health, meanwhile, consuming away and her spirits, which had been so high, utterly broken.

Oh, how often she repented of her folly. How, when she heard of others of her sex forming clandestine marriages; she would shudder and exclaim, "Alas! the chances are that they will be miserable as I am. Can they not see that the man who persuades them to disobey their parents, shows in that very thing a want of principle that promises little for their future happiness!"

But the cup of her misery was not yet full. She had been married a little over a year when her husband left her to visit a neighboring city; and though she waited his return long after the promised day, he never came. At last a letter from him was put into her hands, and the missive announced, in the most un-feeling terms, that he had left her forever.

She sank into a swoon and lay for hours before she recov-ered. When she regained her consciousness, it was to shudder at her condition, for she was penniless, with board for many weeks due, and not a friend on whom she could call for the slightest loan. Suddenly the parable of the Prodigal Son came up to her memory.

"I will arise and go to my father," she said, humbly, in the words of that beautiful story; and, with the exclamation she went forth; to seek her home and sue forgiveness, heart-broken as she was.

It was snowing fast, but she did not heed it. She had thrown on a bonnet and a light shawl; but had forgotten to change her thin shoes, or to assume a cloak. The melting flakes penetrated her slight attire, but she hurried on, breasting the wild tempest.

She arrived at last in the proud square where her father lived, and stood a few moments after in front of the house.

The window shutters were still open, though twilight had set in, and through the curtains the ruddy glow of the fire within shot athwart the stormy night.

A sharp pain twitched her in the heart; she felt pain, and staggering up the steps just managed to pull the bell, when consciousness departed from her.

The servant who answered the door, started and cried out when she saw apparently a lifeless corpse lying on the step, with the fast falling snow rapidly covering it; and Mr. and Mrs. Warren, who were sitting by the parlor fire, coming out to learn the cause of the disturbance, staggered to behold in the emaciated form, their disobedient child.

They took her in, they wrapped her in warm clothing, they laid her on her own bed; but it was no avail. She revived just enough to ask their forgiveness, and receive it from them weeping. Then murmuring blessings on them she died.

This may be thought a fancy sketch; but it is not. It may be thought an excessive case, it is not that either. Caroline Collins, or Warren, as we would rather call her, was early delivered from her sufferings; and in that, terrible as death may seem to the young and happy, she was blessed. There are others, victims of runaway matches, who drag out an existence so miserable that the grave itself would be a relief.

But as the Scripture impressively says: they that sow the whirlwind, shall reap the storm.

And with that, it was the turn of the others to cry. Especially Mary Ann, who for a time had fancied a man who very much resembled Collins. But after the facts of the matter had been explained to her by her father, she had thought better of it. She now had her eye on a preacher named James Reagan, whom she would soon capture. Was Mary Ann crying because of what she thought was a narrow escape, or was she crying because deep down she still loved the wayward lad? No one, least of all her parents, and perhaps even Mary Ann, would ever know.

11

"Tolerably Black"

"Henry, this is almost certainly a waste of time and money. And it is my own damned fault. Lettin' that boy have a free pass and not watchin' him like I should have. But I guess I ought to give it a try. What needs to go in the ad?"

A sheepish Montraville Weaver was addressing a clerk at the *Asheville News* office in June of 1858. He had finally, and with the greatest reluctance, come to the conclusion that his slave, Mingo, had run away.

"Mr. Weaver, just describe him to me and I'll write it down and put it in the notice."

"Well, let's see, we reckon he is around 20 years old, about 150 pounds and 5 feet eight inches high. Thick, bushy hair, kind of a down look, oh, and he has a small scar on his left cheek."

"Is he well-spoken?"

"Not really. Truth be told he rarely spoke. Always seemed tongue-tied. Wait a minute, he has a bit of a lisp."

"What sort of shade of black would you say he is?"

"Never thought about that. He's black."

"So he isn't yellow or tawny or coppery? I've had all sorts of descriptions of runaways here. Dark black, very black, jet black, pitch black, blue black, charcoal black, tolerably black, obnoxiously black. Any of those strike you as accurate?"

"Well, let's just go with tolerably black."

"And you say he has a free pass?"

"Yes, and all it said was: This boy has my permission to pass and repass and, you know, please to let him go about my business, with no date or place. He was carryin' a message from me to James Patton who was up at his hotel in Warm Springs. Mingo was supposed to spend the night and return. I just got word from James that the boy never showed up. So he's either skedaddled or come to some mischief. And I'm thinkin' he has skedaddled because the other slaves told me he took along his Bible and more clothes than he would need on an overnight trip."

"Has he ever run off before? I know some of them darkies like to take their chance and visit with kinfolk on other farms or just blow off steam for awhile and return?"

"He never has done that. If there's a need for one of my slaves to go somewhere I let 'em. I give them a pass. And they've always come back.

"Although there was that time awhile back that one of my slaves, Peter, and one of my brother's slaves, Cato, took it into their heads to try to run off with a pair of my negro gals. But they were really both my brother's slaves. I only took Peter on because James convinced me the pair would be fine if they were separated. Then they got their sorry asses drowned in the French Broad with two of my horses and a pair belonging to James."

"Oh yes, I remember that little episode. It was the talk of the town. Pity about the horses.

"Right, then, it does sound like your Mingo has gone, and probably left the area. He could be in another county by now. It is always a mystery to me when somethin' like this happens. These darkies have no hankerin' for freedom. They have no concept of it; they don't know the meaning of the word. You know that as well as I do. That is why they are our property. They simply can't get along without us showing them the right path.

"And if you don't mind my saying so, I'm thinking that the problem might be that you treated him too well. Have you heard about this mad-doctor down in Louisiana that has a theory about runaways?"

"No, Henry, I have heard of no such thing."

"Well, see, I was talkin' to another clerk here who got it from a ped-dler who I believe saw it in *DeBow's Review*. He told me about this doctor and his theory. Name's Cartwright I think. There's some sick mental state, see, he calls it somethin' scientific, some sort of mania. Anyhow, this sickness is why slaves try to escape. And he says it is caused by masters who become too familiar with their slaves. Says you gotta watch out when they get real sulky and seem dissatisfied for no good reason. And the way to prevent it is a damned hard whippin' at the first sign.

"Now I know you treat your darkies well. Maybe too well? If you were harsher like some I could name, unconstrained to show them the whip, and worse, maybe you wouldn't be havin' this problem. Personally, though, I think the main reason is they just don't like hard work."

"Henry, that all sounds like complete hogwash to me. In the first place, do you really believe negroes have no desire for freedom? What about the free negroes? And the slaves who manage to buy their own freedom? I used to believe, with all my heart, that slaves don't want free-dom, but I've met a fair number of free negroes and not one of them seems to want to go back into bondage. So I'm less and less sure all the time. Oh, with Cato and Peter I understood their motivation all right. They were just womanizers who weren't gettin' what they wanted on the farm. If freedom entered the picture for them, it was just the freedom to fornicate.

"And as for the mental sickness you talked about, that 'doctor' strikes me as a charlatan selling his brand of mental snake oil, tryin' to make a name for himself. Slaves ain't gonna want to run away because they are treated too well. Come on!

"As for Mingo, I don't know. I always thought of him as a good boy, not shiftless like some of the others. And not sulky! And he never gave any overt indication of being clever or independent. But now that I have had some time to think on the matter I have come to the conclusion that it may have all been an act. I believe he has been planning this for some time.

"You know about the slave rebellion in what they now call Haiti? Jane has been reading a book about it that was published in England and she related some interesting passages to me. Seems that the slaves showed an amazing ability to organize themselves and plan their revolt. And they were relentless in pursuing their freedom, utterly ruthless, and bloodthirsty. It does make one think."

"But Mr. Weaver, with all due respect, that would never happen here. I do reckon we can't be too careful with these darkies, not for one moment, but as I understand it, they had a different system down there. Conditions were much worse. The plantation owners were brutal, the slaves were sorely mistreated. Those slaves may have had no choice – they were being worked to death – they were so bad off it was a matter of fight or die. We take care of our negroes. Besides, that was decades ago and nothing even remotely comparable has happened here, especially after the legislature cracked down on them following that bastard Nat Turner's murderous rampage."

"Maybe you are right. Although I have heard dreadful stories about how some of the big cotton growers down South treat their negroes. Shackling, branding, working them 15 or 16 hours a day, everyday, taking advantage of the women, working five year old pickaninnies in the fields. Almost makes me ashamed to be a slaveholder."

"Well all I can say is that all the niggers I encounter around here are docile, obedient, more like a child than a man or woman."

"But don't you think that maybe buried deep down there is this seed that every man and woman has? If not to insurrect, at least to want to be free. And in some, at any rate, that seed is bound to sprout. And that is maybe what happened with Mingo. Anyhow, what I both feel and know is that I want him back."

"Whatever you say, Mr. Weaver. If you are sure you want to do this we can certainly accommodate you. But the odds are not good you know. You are probably wasting your money."

"Yes, I think it is worth a try. Like I said, his ways of speakin' are not going to help him get far, unless he was faking that too. But I think he might be hiding out somewhere close by."

"What is he worth to you?"

"Well, I have $850 invested in him. So I'd like to offer a $50 reward for capture and bringin' him back to me, or puttin' him in jail."

"That will get folks' attention. We can run this ad tomorrow."

"Thank you sir."

And so the ad was placed:

$50 REWARD.

RUNAWAY from the subscriber on the
18th instant, his negro boy

MINGO,

aged 20 years, tolerably black, weighs 150 pounds, 5 feet 8 inches high, rather tongue-tied and lisps slightly, thick bushy head of hair, rather a down look, and has a small scar on the left cheek. Said boy is suspected to have a free pass. The above reward will be paid for his capture and delivery to me, or confinement in any Jail so that I get him.

M. M. WEAVER
Reems Creek P.O., Buncombe co, June 24, 1858

This was the only time Montraville Weaver had had to resort to such a measure. Because aside from the episode with Cato and Peter his slaves had always been submissive and dutiful, at least when he was around. Yes, there had been the usual malingering and lackadaisical work, but he had decided to just put up with it as long as it wasn't taken too far.

On the other hand, maybe that sort of thing was getting worse. He had noticed lately, which tended to push him nearly over the edge, field hands seeming to spend the greater part of the day loafing around, picking the occasional ear of corn, and then just before the end of the day engaging in a slapdash effort to make up for their idleness. This impressive-to-look-at all-out effort left them breathless but accomplished little, as an inspection of the fields would demonstrate: the easy pickings gone and the areas harder to reach untouched. He had spoken to George about it but even he basically would just shrug his shoulders.

What especially rankled was the ingratitude of his slaves. And that went double for Mingo. Montraville increasingly viewed his slaves and, frankly, slavery in general with little enthusiasm. But he was certain there was no alternative.

He did believe that his slaves were unable to fend for themselves. Oh, there were certainly exceptions, maybe Mingo was one, maybe George was another, but in his opinion, which was shared by whites throughout the South (and he felt, the North as well), the average slave was incapable of managing his or her life. They had to be looked after. On their own, they would not know what to do and would either perish from a lack of the means to get from one day to the next, or turn to a life of crime.

Before the disappearance, Montraville had been certain that such was the case with Mingo, who had never shown the least bit of initiative or even common sense. He could vividly recall how Mingo, when told that he needed to take a message to Warm Springs, seemed to have a great deal of difficulty understanding the most basic instructions. Montraville had had to explain over and over, in minute detail, what the boy was supposed to do and how he was supposed to do it. But now Montraville, assuming that Mingo indeed was a runaway and was not wandering aimlessly around goodness knows where, was beginning to feel that maybe, just maybe, Mingo was much cleverer than he could ever have guessed.

At any rate, by the time the ad appeared in the *Asheville News*, Mingo, in truth, was long gone. Because after heading a short distance toward Patton's hotel, he had struck out for what he believed would be a refuge and his pathway to freedom.

Since he had been taken on by Montraville through an estate sale, Mingo had made it his business never to seem rebellious in any way or give the impression that he could in fact fend for himself. He knew Montraville was a smart man, but he was also convinced that he could outsmart him. He had worked just hard enough to avoid George's and his master's displeasure, while hatching a scheme to make his escape. For he had heard from Daniel, a field slave on a neighboring farm, about Nigger Mountain.

There were lots of tales in those days about that black granite hill which abruptly rose 1600 feet above the flatland south of Jefferson. It was supposedly chock-full of caves beneath its ledges where a man could hide out for as long as he wanted, and there were supposedly free Negroes and good white folks that would leave food and clothing for runaways. There was even talk that a station on the Underground Railroad was located in the vicinity.

Mingo had also been told that Nigger Mountain was like a beacon and that a traveler headed north could not miss it. In reality, yes, it stood out for sure, but if one was unfamiliar with the area, it might well look a lot like all the other "mountains." And, it was nearly 100 miles northeast, as the crow flew. And Mingo was no crow. And the route was nearly all up and down, with rivers and streams in the way.

Fortunately, Mingo, unlike most slaves, knew how to swim. His mama, before they were separated, had thrown him in a lake not long after he had learned to walk. He had taken every opportunity to spend time in the water thereafter. Also, Daniel had explained to Mingo how to fashion a raft in the event that crossing a wide body of water became necessary.

"You go find some fence rails, at least six to be on the safe side. Tie 'em together with whatever rope you can find, or failin' that a strong vine. When you has made the crossing, separate the rails and send 'em downstream, leavin' no sign that you was ever there."

Daniel had made a break for freedom some years before, but had made it only a couple of dozen miles toward his goal before being intercepted by a slave patrol and returned to his owner. The 25 lashes a day he had received for four straight days, as well as what he now regarded as the impossibility of escape, convinced him to toe the mark, or at least pretend to. He actually counted himself lucky not to have been sold on to some plantation farther south where he would have had to pick cotton all day.

"Mingo," he would say, "I knows all about this dream of your'n, 'cause I had it too. But listen to me: give it up. You has no chance. Tell me Mingo, why does you want to do this? Are you in trouble with Mr. Weaver? I hear tell he ain't such a bad boss. And he don't seem to keep you on such a tight rein. Seems like you is always comin' over here to bother me. You might want to give this a little more thought, 'cause when you git caught I can guarantee you things will git a whole lot worse for you."

Mingo, of course, was not listening. "I knows the odds ain't good, but I'se young, and strong, and smart. So you can jest forget about tryin' to stop me and start tellin' me what I need to know to make this happen."

And that is just what Daniel did. In reality, he was not about to discourage anyone else who might have the dream of freedom. He just wanted to make sure that Mingo was truly driven to make the attempt, that it was not just a passing fancy. So Daniel explained about orienting by the North Star, and the necessity to make as quick a start as possible since bloodhounds were useless unless a runaway was still in the area. He drummed into Mingo the need to travel only at night, and to avoid roads whenever possible. Since it was summertime, the nights were short, which was a bit of a disadvantage because it would limit the time Mingo could travel and certainly prolong the journey. But the warm weather would obviously be advantageous.

And when Mingo came to him one evening and told him he would be taking a message to the hotel in Warm Springs, and that this was the chance he had been waiting for, Daniel related what he had learned about a route that another slave had passed on to him in preparation for his escape attempt. "Start out toward the hotel, but afore you git to Lapland, there's a road off to the right that kinda follows Ivy Creek. Keep headin' in that general direction and you'll come to Pleasant Hill where you can cut back south. Head toward Black Dome, but stay below it. Follow the valley divide, keepin' to the west, until you see the Ginger-Cake Rocks. Know what I'm talkin' about?"

"You know full well I hasn't the least idea."

"They are rocks piled up on what they call Ginger-Cake Mountain, piled upside down, more than 50 foot high I would say. Smallest rocks on the bottom and a huge slab on top. It is about the strangest thing I has ever seen. Unfortunately that is where the patrol caught me, admiring those rocks. You can see them from miles away. So anyhow, there you will find a road headin' straight toward Boone. Stay away from the road but go along it, and be sure to stay south of Boone. Then you can pretty much follow the New River straight north to Nigger Mountain, which you can't miss. It is black as pitch."

"How the hell do you think I'm goin' to be able to find these roads and these rivers?"

"To tell the truth, I don't. I think you are never goin' to find Nigger Mountain and are never goin' to be free. But I ain't gonna tell you not to go. Just keep followin' the star and maybe it will light the way for you. And one more bit of advice – trust no one. Includin' other niggers – there's them that won't hesitate for one second turnin' you in for whatever piddlin' little reward they might hope to receive."

In preparation for his break for freedom, Mingo had squirreled away some food and whatever extra clothing he could muster, although since it was summer he wouldn't be needing much. And the following day he was ready.

The first part was easy of course. After all, he was a fully authorized messenger with a free pass. But then, when he turned off the route to the Warm Springs Hotel, hesitating just for a second or two, he instantly became a fugitive. And he knew nothing would be easy from then on.

The trek toward Nigger Mountain was every bit as difficult as Daniel had described. The only thing that Mingo was certain of was that he was going in generally the right direction. Days and nights passed in which there was hardly anything to eat, and little if any progress was made.

Once, he became feverish and had to hole up for three days, awakening on the third day from a frightening dream. In the dream he had been asleep, deep in the woods, when a man and a boy, out hunting, had spotted him lying down, fast asleep.

The man told the boy, apparently his son: "Well, well. What has we here? Must be a runaway. This indeed is our lucky day. Maybe we ain't found no game, but looks like we just bagged us a runaway nigger."

As he pointed his rifle at Mingo and prepared to wake him, the son said: "Daddy, cain't we just let him lay there? Come on, let's go back home. I think we should just leave him be."

"Son, are you crazy? Do you know how much money we can git for him?"

"But it ain't right!"

"You been listenin' to that preacher too much. I told your Ma he was a bad influence. With all that 'do unto others' nonsense."

"Please, Daddy, let's just go."

"Son, he's a nigger, not a real man like you intend to be. And if we don't turn him in, someone else sure as shootin' will."

But the tears welling up in his son's eyes carried the day, and grudgingly the man let himself be led away.

That is when Mingo woke up, shaking himself awake from what he would come to recall as the most vivid dream he had ever had. And the one he was able to remember in some detail, unlike most other dreams. Later he would come to question whether or not it was a dream. But it must have been. No white man would turn down the chance to cash in on his black body. Yet, it did seem so real in retrospect.

That was about the time his fever broke, and that night he was able to cover several miles on a deserted road with nobody in sight. Most of the time, however, he was not as fortunate. The days were interminable -- being able to move hardly at all for fear of discovery and beset by insects and snakes. There were times he was so frustrated with inactivity that he risked moving during the day, when the foliage was comfortingly thick and, he hoped, there was little chance that anyone would be in the area. The problem, though, was that this was not only extremely dangerous, but also exhausting. So he couldn't then take full advantage of the nights. But moving in the day or the night, he only had one thing on his mind. Every step he took was bringing him closer to freedom.

Much time was spent searching for something, anything, to eat. The best times were when he came upon a farmhouse with a garden plot and he could lie low and, when he was able to detect no light coming from the house, avail himself of whatever vegetables and potatoes he found there. Only once was he so careless as to arouse the household. But fortunately the farmer's aim was poor and he did not have dogs.

But the incident prompted Mingo to think about the possibility that the farmer would alert the slave patrols and go after him. So he decided to cross a wide nearby river he had been following, whatever river it in fact was, and think about building and utilizing the raft that Daniel had talked about. Only problem was: there were no likely looking fence rails anywhere about, and certainly no rope, nor strong vines. So Mingo decided the best course of action was to just swim across. There didn't seem to be much of a current, and he felt he might be able to walk much of the way, and there was no one about. So that is what he did. All the time saying thank you to his mama for throwing him in the lake all those years earlier. And then, after resting for a short while, he was on his way again. Following the North Star.

Some nights he made almost no progress. Cloud-filled nights were especially dispiriting, inasmuch as Mingo could not be certain he was even headed in the right direction, except on the rare occasions when he was keeping within sight of a road or stream that he was sure, or as sure as he could be, was heading north.

And no matter how hungry or sick or tired he might be, he knew taking a gamble on encountering another human being, white or black, whether for food, shelter, or directions, was exceedingly risky. He had glimpsed, from a distance, in some dusty town south of Boone, a coffle of runaways, or rather attempted runaways, fettered together, apparently being herded back south to the slaves' owners.

They were about the sorriest bunch of Negroes he had ever seen. Dirty, thin, dressed in rags, with blank expressions that said to him: "Do not get caught, whatever you do, or whatever you have to do." Maybe the sight should have frightened him, but in truth all it did was make him more determined. He might be hungry, exhausted, scared much of the time, and grievously lonely, but he knew there was no turning back. At any rate, the loneliness he could bear. Separated from his mother and siblings as a child, he had taken care never to grow attached to anyone.

He was comfortable in his own black skin. And he was realizing more and more every day that he could deal with the rest of his troubles.

By the time he saw what he was sure was Nigger Mountain he had lost much weight, and he looked and felt exceedingly frail. But he hastened the last few miles, climbed as far up as he could in his weakened condition, found a cave, and slept for two days and nights.

When he awoke, he looked around his hideout for the first time, and was not sure if he liked what he saw. Clearly there had been people there before him, many people. Telltale signs of previous human occupation were everywhere. Footprints, improvised bedding, an old campfire. Unfortunately, however, there was no food. Lots of chestnut husks. So apparently there were chestnut trees somewhere. Whoever had been there before him must have roasted the chestnuts. Mingo, on his trek, had made attempts to eat them raw, which left him frustrated and, to the extent that he was able to access and nibble on the fruit, sick to his stomach.

He was understandably parched and starving. Cautiously leaving his shelter, he was able to find rocky outcrops which held plentiful rainwater. Food was obviously going to be a bigger concern. There were a few straggly red mulberry and wild blackberry bushes. And, near the summit, he found numerous chestnut trees, but there was no way to cook the chestnuts. He dared not start a fire, even if he had had the means.

Back in the cave, he was considering his options when he heard, from some distance, voices. Were they coming closer? Yes, they were definitely coming closer. If they were bounty hunters or slave-catchers, it was all over. And even if they were other Negroes, the words of his friend to trust no one were ringing in his ears. But what could he do? He had no way to defend himself, and nowhere to go. The men were coming up the same way he had, and he knew that if he tried to make a break for it, in his weakened condition they would have no problem collaring him.

He had no choice but to retreat into the cave and try to hide.

And there, flattening himself as best he could against the wall of the cave for what seemed like an eternity, he listened as the men approached. They were no longer talking. Had they somehow worked out that there was someone there? Even the sounds of his pursuers, for that is what he now thought they must be, making their way toward him seemed to be muffled. But was that a twig being stepped on? Or a branch snapping back after someone moved through the bushes? Were those whispers he was hearing? Or just leaves rustling in the breeze?

And then, almost before he knew it, the men were there, crouching down in the mouth of the cave. With the sun behind them, Mingo could not see what they looked like, or for that matter whether they were black or white. It appeared that one was tall and one quite short. And the taller one had something, maybe a stick, or maybe a rifle, that he was pointing into the cave. Then he heard them speak, very softly.

"Avery, someone is in here. Move away and keep back, in case he is armed."

"Paw, over toward the right, half way down that side. Yesss! Someone's peepin' out from where the wall juts out."

This of course caused Mingo to attempt to flatten himself against the wall, but to the intruders that only made it more obvious that someone was indeed hiding.

"Son, keep down!" And to the shadowy figure he had seen: "I have me a rifle and it is ready to fire. Come on out and I want to see empty hands."

Now Mingo saw that he had no choice. His only hope was that they were not bounty hunters or slave-catchers. He edged away from his hiding place, hands in front of him, empty of course, and with some considerable relief saw a tall black man with nothing but a cane in his hands.

"Hey there mister, it's all right. We come in peace," said the man, nearly as relieved as Mingo. "My name is Archibald. And my son, come on over boy, is Avery. We're free negroes from a few miles south and every so often we come up here to see if anyone needs help. And unless I am mistaken indeed, we have found someone who needs help. You a runaway?"

"Yessir" he muttered as he crept slowly forward. Then somewhat more forcefully as he tried to convince himself that everything was going to be okay he answered: "And I does need help. Does you have anythin' to eat?"

"Avery, give this man some of that corn bread and bacon we brought."

Mingo thought that he had never heard sweeter words. As the lad pulled the victuals from his pack and handed him the food Mingo fell to his knees and wasted no time in eating his fill. Then, scrambling to his feet, he washed it down with some smooth corn whiskey that Archibald produced.

"Whoa, take it easy there! Don't make yourself sick," warned Archibald. "There's more where that came from. So anyhow who are you and where did you come from?"

"My name is Mingo. I been here two days arter walkin' for weeks and weeks from way down south, near Asheville. I'se been tol' that this here mountain is a spot where I might find help so's I can git on up north to freedom."

"Mingo, happy to make your acquaintance. That is indeed a long trek. And we will do what we can to help you out. But, while there are people, other people I mean, besides us, who can help, there are also plenty of folks that mean you harm, and will do whatever it takes to hunt you down and turn you in to the authorities, or worse.

"Most of the white folks in these parts are unenthusiastic toward slavery and in no great sympathy with the slaveholders. But, the slaveholders have pretty much all the wealth in the county, and all the power. It is said that one of the worst of the lot, Colonel Bower, owns a thousand acres and dozens of slaves. He basically controls what goes on in this county. And every once in awhile he gets together with the other slave-holders and they hire some low-lifes to help them hunt black folks down, and one of the areas they always like to search is this mountain.

"You ain't gonna want to hear this, but we has learned that some of them folks are likely to be here searching this area real soon. We has made the acquaintance of two of Colonel Bower's slaves. And they have been overhearing conversations between him and other slaveholders about what they is calling a raid on this here mountain. That is why we is here. To see if we could find any runaways and warn them that they should be on their way.

"This here cave, which we call 'Moonshiner's Cave,' has been used right often, and we know it well. But so do the slaveholders and slave-catchers. You is just plain lucky that we found you afore they did. My advice to you, because we can't take you with us, it is too dangerous, for us and you, is for you to find a spot some distance off — there's a place we call Luther Rock, over toward the east end of the ridge — and rest up only as long as you feel the need. And then get the hell out of here. We has some more food we brought with us and you can have all of that. If possible, we will get back here with more provisions for the next part of your journey. But those ruffians may come around any day, so you need to decide quickly what you want to do."

"Mr. Archibald, I has already decided, don't you worry! I'm headin' north as soon as possible. Can you show me the way?"

"'Fraid not, Mingo. Headin' north from here is a sure fire way to get yourself caught, or worse. Southwest Virginia abounds in patrols that have been known to shoot first and never bother to ask questions. And from what I've heard, there is not one white man or woman that has any sympathy for our race. I don't dare go there at all, even though I am free. I'm sorry to have to tell you but, you are goin' to have to head east instead of north.

"There's a Quaker community in Guilford County, a place called New Garden, near a booming town called Greensborough. Has you ever heard of these places?"

Mingo didn't have to think long or hard on the answer to that question. "I know nothin' 'bout any of that. What is a .... quaker?"

"It would take too long to explain their beliefs and customs, but let's just say they have no use for slavery and want to abolish it and make all negro men and women free. There are lots of people there who will provide food, clothing, and shelter, and guide you to wherever you want to go. However, it is still a long way off. Anyhow, we need to discuss this further but first we must find you a better hiding spot. Follow us.

"Avery, lead the way."

"Sure thing pa." And without another word, the three, with Archibald's son in the lead, headed off on something resembling a trail, that only someone intimately familiar with the mountain would know about. After an hour or so of difficult hiking, with much scrambling over huge boulders, they came to an outcropping of amphibolite rock, with a view which stretched for miles.

"Mingo, there are lots of crannies here where you should be able to rest up and hide if need be. But I am goin' to show you the way you want to go to find the folks who can help you get to safety. Look where I'm pointin'. See that mountain just there? Ain't much of a mountain but that is what folks calls it."

"Yessir, I sees it."

"It is named Cross Mountain. Keep that in view when you head down off this here mountain. When you get there, stay to the right and you will find a stream. It is called Roten Creek. It goes just past Cross Mountain. By the way, I'm tellin' you these names not 'cause you'll need 'em, but 'cause I hope it will help you remember the route you has to take. Anyhow, that stream, Roten Creek, flows into the Reddis River. And that is what you need to follow because it goes in the direction you need to go, southeast, until it smacks into a bigger river called the Yadkin, north of a town called Wilkesboro, after about twenty miles. Stay well clear of Wilkesboro; there are too many bad folks there. But follow the Yadkin as it flows east, downstream.

"The Yadkin twists and turns. Just keep following it until you see, on your left, maybe five or six miles off, about the strangest mountain you will ever see. It's called Pilot Mountain. Trees cover it, see, but then up near the top are bare rock walls, and then more trees and bushes on the very summit. It sure looks like a woman's teat. There is no way you can miss it. Anyhow, when you see that and are pretty much due south of it, go another five miles or so. That is where the river turns south. You need to leave the river there and keep headin' east. Follow the risin' sun. Look, with great caution, for a settlement called Salem.

"There's a community of what are called Moravians there. Most of the white folks are farmers who own slaves, but the slaves have some ability to move around, and there are plenty of free negroes there as well. Again, be careful of the whites, but you should be able to get help and more specific directions from the negroes. If you decide to bypass Salem, just keep headin' due east, oh, about twenty miles more and you will need to look for that place I told you about, New Garden. There's a meeting house there used by those Quakers. And if anyone can, they will find a way to get you to safety.

"Now have you got all that? Give it back to me."

He hadn't gotten all that, not even close, but after Archibald went through it a few more times, asking Mingo to repeat the route, he was eventually able to pass the test. However, Mingo still needed some convincing.

"Mr. Archibald, I ain't sure I can do this. I barely escaped with my life comin' here, and arrived nearly starvin.'"

"Mingo, you has no choice. As I said, it would be suicide to head on north from here. But a month's journey to the east you will find a group of people who know how to get you where you want to go, safely. I've met them. You can trust anyone at the Quaker meeting house, but ask for Mr. Alfred Coffin, actually anybody named Coffin, or Mr. Andrew Murrow. They are well able to hide escapees like you and send you on your way to freedom through what they call the Underground Railroad."

"I'se heard of that. So there really is such a thing?"

"Oh yes! Of course it ain't really underground and it ain't really a railroad. But there is a line set up with stations, mostly just folks' homes and businesses, and good people manning those stations. They will help find you a place of safety. There are lots of ways they do that.

"You might be able to hide in special places where no one would think to look for you. There is a disguised room at Mr. Murrow's farm-yard, behind stacks of feed. I has also seen a wagon with a false bottom which Murrow drives up north to Indiana, selling corn meal and pottery in the bed of the wagon on the way. I also understand that a woman named Vina Curry lets escapees use her dead husband's free papers to make their way north. Indeed, there is a whole network of good people, Quakers and otherwise, that provides assistance."

"Alright Mr. Archibald, but I doesn't know if I can do it. I'se right tired of bein' hungry and cold and dirty and worst of all, scared all the time." And he hung his head and the tears started flowing. Archibald grabbed him around the shoulders and put his arms around him.

"Mingo, you can do it. Trust me, if you can walk from way down south, through the mountains, to this place, you can get to New Garden. And there you will find the best folks in the land, who will get you to freedom.

"Now we need to get back home ourselves. There's a massive storm a-comin' for sure. And we is free negroes, but all that means is that if the white folks don't mind the look of you, and if they ask for your papers and find them in order, they might let you go about your business. Avery, leave the rest of the food we brought. That'll get Mingo off to a good start. And remember Mingo, do not delay. I reckon that as soon as the storm passes, Bower and his cronies, or his hired riffraff, will be here.

"And Mingo, you can eat the mayapples, which I see have turned yellow and taste real good. We will be taking what we can carry back home. The wife loves 'em. But make sure you remove the seeds. Stay away from the other plants, especially the ivybush and rosebay. They will certainly make you sick. And so will the chestnuts unless you roast 'em. Take this knife, which will make it easier to remove the seeds from the mayapples. And you never know when else it will come in handy."

This started Mingo crying again. But with a mighty effort he managed to pull himself together, grab Archibald's hand and, in a strained voice, declare that "I thanks you, more than you can ever know, for your help. Now, you had best be on your way, before it gets any darker."

And without another word being said, the man and the boy disappeared into the rhododendron and mountain laurel thicket, and were gone from Mingo's sight in an instant.

The storm that Archibald predicted arrived soon thereafter. It rained as heavily as Mingo had seen it on his journey, but he was able to find a spot underneath one of the ledges, where he could stay mostly dry and screw up his courage so he would be able to move off the mountain and down toward the Reddis River.

Then on the afternoon of the following day, after the storm had abated, he heard men's voices, shouting and laughing, from the direction of Moonshiner's Cave. Had they found some unfortunate? Were they on his tail? No way to tell, but Mingo figured it was past time to be on his way.

It was hard to scramble down the mountain without making noise and Mingo thought for sure it would alert what he assumed were his pursuers. And then, when he got to the base of the mountain, what had seemed like an easy enough landmark to find, Cross Mountain, was heaven knows where? Things looked completely different to him. But he kept telling himself to calm down and looking back he was able to see about where he had come from and use that to pick out the mountain he was headed to.

And the best part of that look back was not seeing anyone coming after him.

But, the slave-catchers had noticed him, from a distance, and presumed he was a runaway. They were occupied in dealing with another escapee they had discovered on the mountain and would report what they had seen to the Colonel when they took the man, in chains, horse-whipped, back to Bowers' estate.

The Colonel would want to know what the man knew about the other man who had fled down the mountain and he would not believe him when the man said he had not seen or met the other. Bower would bring out his own whip in an attempt to learn the truth. And then order that the black man be taken to the Jefferson courthouse, where he would be thrown, more dead than alive, into the jail. Would Bower then order his underlings to take off after the escapee, or would he, taking it into his head that it would be great fun to chase down that nigger, order his rig be brought around so he could find and deal with the man himself? We shall never know for sure.

What we do know is that Colonel Bower departed this life when, against his driver-slave's advice, he ordered that his carriage be driven across Brown's ford over a rain-swollen Yadkin River, apparently in pursuit of a runaway slave. Was it Mingo? Would Mingo make it to New Garden? Would the Underground Railroad successfully transport him to Indiana, or New York, or Canada? Or would he be nabbed by a slave catcher and returned to Montraville, or worse? The answers to those questions, like so many others, have been lost in the fog of history.

1 2

"Driven On By the Devil"

Coleman Campbell, the presiding elder of the Methodist Episcopal Church, South's Franklin District, was a tall, broad-shouldered man with a booming yet mellifluent voice, who seemed always in command, whether in the pulpit or at the dinner table. When preaching, it often-times appeared that his congregation was under a spell from the first words out of his mouth. One would be hard-pressed to say whether this was due to the words he spoke or the way he spoke them. But even around a dinner table discussing routine arrangements for the next camp meeting, he displayed an eloquence that could not help but impress his listeners.

An occasional visitor to the farm of Montraville Weaver, he was of course seated next to Jane at dinner, but perhaps paid less attention to what she might have to say than would be expected of a guest. Rather, he was more inclined to pontificate about the affairs of the Church. On one such instance, in the late spring of 1859, he was happily displaying the inside knowledge he had acquired through his elevated ecclesiastical po-sition when he seemed to hesitate mid-sentence and closely observe a black girl who was helping to serve dinner.

This was Easter, a young field slave. She had just placed a bowl of soup in front of Montraville, who was sitting across the table. Easter was still in her teens, but had filled-out nicely in the past year and had a cur-vaceous, womanly body that even the plainest dress could not mask. It did not escape the attention of either Jane or Montraville that Camp-bell's eyes would stray to Easter throughout the meal, whether he was in the process of revealing the latest Methodist Conference gossip or asking one of the children to pass the peas.

After dinner, Campbell seemed to linger at the table, in spite of the fact that he had a fair distance to travel to Alexander's Stand and had been saying earlier how much he was looking forward to spending the night there. "They always treat me right" he had exclaimed, "and their smithy is the best (and the cheapest) I've encountered in three states." Jane feared the man was angling to sleep under her roof. But eventually, with a backward glance at the door through which Easter has some time earlier exited the dining room, Campbell departed.

Later, Jane would mention to her husband how uneasy Campbell's barely disguised interest in the girl made her feel.

"Mont, you know I have heard rumors about Mr. Campbell and his relations with young women of both races. You are I am certain much better informed. Should we be worried?"

Montraville had heard those rumors himself, from what he considered reliable sources, but he chose to put his wife off with some words to the effect that she should not give any credence to gossip surrounding the clergy. Such things were inevitable. But in truth, Montraville was concerned, albeit not ready to admit it to Jane. He felt he could take care of the matter.

He had never much cared for Campbell, who he had long ago decided was not an original thinker. Even Campbell himself would admit that in truth he was neither a reader nor a student. Most of his sermons owed far more to others than to his own intellect. He didn't exactly plagiarize; he was much too clever for that. But Montraville frequently detected the efforts of other ministers (including himself) in Campbell's sermons. Montraville even recalled the day that Jane, listening to Campbell preaching about the Sermon on the Mount, had turned to him and whispered: "Is not this what you were saying at the dinner table the other day? The good elder has turned it into a prose poem."

117

She was correct. Campbell had taken his host's words and rephrased them, thrown in a couple of not-very-relevant anecdotes, wound things up with an emotional peroration, and, in Montraville's opinion at any rate, ended up creating more heat than light.

"Jane, I'm beginning to think that Mr. Campbell only opens the Bible when he is conducting a service, and that he otherwise has no use for it. But his oratory certainly impresses folks," answered Montraville.

As it happened, Campbell was again in the area only a few weeks later, on Independence Day. It would be a sweltering day, as it should be for that glorious occasion. Jane and Montraville would be paying their annual visit to his brother, James, born on the Fourth of July sixty-five years before, dead nearly five years and buried near Paint Rock on the old Catawba Trail. It was so sad to think about James and how he loved that day of the year! What celebrations the family had enjoyed!

John and Kittie went along on the journey; they hadn't been to the grave since the day James was buried. Jane was feeling poorly and Montraville suggested she not join the party, but she wouldn't hear of it. She also insisted on stopping to view the pictographs, large red and yellow geometric figures, which gave the area its name.

"Mont, is it my imagination or were these much more vivid when we first came here all those years ago?"

"Jane, I do believe you are correct. But perhaps it is more our memories that have faded, and not the paintings?"

Upon their return, hot, exhausted and sad, they discovered Coleman Campbell nosing around the slave quarters.

"Why Mr. Campbell, sir, it is, of course, always a pleasure to see you, but I do think you should have notified me that you were planning on visiting. Then I could have been here to receive you properly. Can I help you with something?" said Montraville.

Campbell replied: "I just happened to be passing through and thought I would pay a visit. And since I was here, I thought it would be a kindness to say a prayer of comfort with your slaves."

"Well, and since you are here, would you like to join us for our Independence Day celebration?"

"I would truly like nothing better, but unfortunately I have business I have to attend to up the road," he answered.

"That is a great pity Mr. Campbell," replied Montraville. "It is going to be quite a shindig. Anyhow, I would like to remind you that it would be very greatly appreciated if you would notify me when you intend to drop by, and I would ask that you never stop by when I am not here. These negroes are my responsibility in matters of both faith and conduct, and I do not want anyone playing favorites, shall we say, or upsetting them in any way."

If the elder took offense at this he made no show of it, simply tipping his hat, mounting his horse, and riding away.

Montraville spoke to Easter later. She was a shy girl who generally kept to herself and, as far as he knew, had never taken up with any of the men at his farm or those nearby. She had of course heard Campbell preach and as with everybody else no doubt had been impressed by him.

"Easter, what was Mr. Campbell doing here? Did he speak to you?"

The response was disquieting. "The Reverend brought me a patriotic shawl. Leastwise, that's what he called it. Here 'tis."

The thing was festooned with a scraggly eagle, perhaps remotely resembling the symbol of the American nation, along with flowers that appeared to have seen better days. It was one of the ugliest shawls, if that is what it actually was, that Montraville had ever seen. But he chose not to share this viewpoint with Easter.

"Did he bring anything for the others?" he asked.

Easter shook her head.

"Has he been here to see you before?"

Easter this time hesitated before, with obvious reluctance, nodding. "Did he bring you gifts before?"

"Jest some beads. Some prayer beads, he called 'em."

"And I assume he has not brought gifts for any of the others?"

Again Easter reluctantly nodded.

"Did he touch you? Has he ever touched you? Tell me the truth now."

Easter shook her head. But did Montraville again sense a slight hesitation on her part? He needed to be sure. "Where did he touch you?"

This time Easter shook her head and cried out: "He didn't touch me anywhere! He is a godly man. He wouldn't!"

Montraville found this somewhat less than reassuring, given his doubts about the man's "godliness."

Still, he needed to remain calm. Campbell was an important man in the Conference, and there was no proof that he had any lecherous interest in Easter.

"All right. If you say so. But I have my doubts about his intentions. It is clear that he wanted to see you and had no interest in the others," said Montraville. "If you see him again, at any time, come to me, or to John or to your mistress if I am not here. If he comes when we are all away, join the others in their cabin and do not go anywhere alone with Mr. Campbell."

Montraville was worried. He asked John and Jane to keep their eyes open for anything suspicious and to let him know right away, and to come get him if necessary, if Campbell showed up again. He had a mighty suspicion that he would.

But he was not about to let Coleman Campbell cast a pall on the Independence Day celebration. There was roasted chicken, parsnips, poke sallet, and corn pudding. The girls recited the Declaration of Independence and sang some songs. It almost made Montraville forget the somber journey to Paint Rock and Campbell's unsettling appearance.

However, he could not help thinking that there might not be many more such celebrations.

Thomas Lanier Clingman, a notorious firebrand and recently elected United States Senator from just up the road in Asheville, had again been spouting those secessionist views of his, trying to whip everybody up: "Do us justice and we stand with you; attempt to trample on us and we separate!" So far, only a select few seemed to be buying that line, at least in North Carolina, or at least in western North Carolina, thought Montraville, but who could tell what was going to happen? Word was out that the hopeless James Buchanan was not going to run again. Who would? He only prayed that it would be someone who could deal with the secessionists and fashion some sort of compromise.

In any case, Montraville thoroughly enjoyed the day's festivities and was able to put his troubles at least temporarily to the side. But then, two days later, things with Campbell got completely out of hand. Sometime in the night Montraville heard a commotion at the stable. Quickly lighting two lanterns, he woke John and together they quietly exited the rear of the house. Agitated voices could be heard some distance off, seemingly a male and female voice. Montraville and John advanced slowly, straining to make out what the pair was saying.

John said: "It's a man and a woman for sure, and I think she's saying 'No, no, no....'"

"Without a doubt," replied Montraville, "and I fear the man is not listening."

Sure enough, Campbell was there with Easter, and he had his arms around her and seemed to be attempting to raise her shift. When Montraville shined the light on them, Campbell, startled as if just awakened, backed away and, gathering his wits about him, said "I'm praying with her. She's a wicked child and needs the Lord's help."

Seeing Easter quivering and obviously unsure what to do, Montraville asked if she was able to return to her quarters and suggested that she do so, adding "I'll talk to you later."

"Mister Campbell, I need you to come into the house with me. Now!" ordered Montraville. "John, come with us. I want you to hear our discussion."

"You can't talk that way to me," sputtered Campbell. "I'm within my rights and you have no entitlement to interfere. I will just be on my way."

"In a pig's eye," responded Montraville. "Get in the kitchen. I have some words to say to you."

And Campbell, disabused of the notion that he could explain away his behavior, and attempting to pull himself together, fixed Montraville with an icy stare and strode towards the house.

Once in the kitchen with Campbell, Montraville could hardly contain his anger. "What did you think you were doing out there, Mr. Campbell, and after dark? If there was any praying going on, I do believe it was poor Easter who was offering silent prayers for the Lord to make you go away. She was frightened and knew full well that you had no business being here."

Campbell replied: "My only intention was to show her the right path, from which she has strayed. She is sinful. Anyone can see that."

"Frankly Mr. Campbell, I have seen no indication that she has strayed, as you put it, and I'm not sure you know the right path now, if you ever did. And I suppose you just happened to be passing and in spite of my previous directions could not resist 'ministering' to the girl without informing me," snarled Montraville. "I am not going to put up with your trickery any longer. If you show up at this house again, uninvited, ever, I will report what I have seen to the Conference."

"Reverend Weaver, that would be most foolish. This is only a misunderstanding."

Montraville answered: "The misunderstanding will be yours if you think I do not mean it. As God is my witness, I will not allow this mischief to continue. John, please show the man out."

And with that, Campbell was escorted off the premises.

The following day Montraville took Easter aside and learned that Campbell had gone to the women's cabin and told her that he needed to talk to her about her faith in Jesus Christ. She was sleepy and confused, but got dressed quickly and followed him to the stables. Campbell had said she was somebody special and that the Lord had special plans for her. He then embraced her and had started caressing her when Montraville and John appeared on the scene.

"He had no right to do that, you do know that don't you?" said Montraville. "If you ever see him around the place in future, scream bloody murder and I will make sure he never shows up again, ever. He thinks I won't take him on, but you can be sure that I will."

He also scolded Bett, who was essentially in charge of the women's cabin, for not alerting anyone to what Campbell had done. But she had of course been afraid to oppose the elder or any white person for that matter.

Montraville was quite certain that he, and Easter, would be seeing Campbell again. The elder was, unfortunately, a type that was familiar to Montraville, and that included church members and even a few preachers. They were only men after all, and powerful men, some of whom thought they could get away with all manner of corruption. And they usually did. Because, in general, female slaves were in constant danger of drawing the unwanted attentions of their white "masters" or others in authority. They were unprotected by the law, and in fact could, and often would, be viewed as the seducers of their attackers and punished severely, by whipping or worse, if they tried to defend themselves.

But Montraville saw things differently. Although his and the Methodist Episcopal Church, South's position was that slavery was a civil and domestic institution regulated by the civil authorities and not a matter for the Church, he took seriously Colossians 4:1 "Masters, be just and fair to your slaves, knowing that you yourselves have a Master in Heaven." Accordingly, he believed that protection from the depredations of the likes of Coleman Campbell was demanded of any slaveholder who followed the word of God.

In any event, a few days later, Montraville was awakened by George. "Massa, Bett just tol' me that Easter has gone off with that Reverend Campbell agin."

"Where did they go?" said Montraville.

"They was headed down the lane toward the parsonage."

Not wanting to get George involved in what was increasingly looking like a war of words, or worse, with a Church elder, Montraville replied: "Go wake up John, then you can return to bed. I'm going to get Jane. We'll find them."

After assembling the search party, and lighting two lanterns, Montraville led the way. "Jane, I find it hard to believe that the man can be so stupid. Does he truly think that just because he is an elder I will let him get away with this?"

She replied: "You know I've never trusted him. He may be a spellbindin' orator, but I think that you can tell he is not deep down a godly person. He is a fraud without a moral bone in his body. You've heard his stories about how the negroes all love him and will do anything for him? Apparently he thinks that applies to carnality as much as anything else. And I'm afraid that Easter is simply not able to resist him – she doesn't know what to do in the company of such an important white man."

John joined in: "He won't be so 'important' when you get through with him, eh Papa?"

"First let's see what exactly he is up to," cautioned Montraville.

As they proceeded quietly down the lane, they started to hear what sounded like sobbing, and a man's voice, saying over and over again, "Be good, Easter." Soon, they were able to detect movement off to the side of the lane. There were two people, the burly elder of the Church with his trousers down around his ankles, his hands gripping his companion's buttocks, and his mouth glued to her right breast, and the pretty young slave with her shift half off her, trying to push him away. Campbell seemed to be in a frenzied state, but as he became aware of light coming from behind him and the sound of footsteps he raised his head and half turned.

"Mr. Campbell, back away," ordered Montraville.

Seeing the pair locked in their unnatural embrace, Jane averted her eyes. John at first could only stare in disbelief, but then, seeing Elder Campbell's stunned expression and state of undress, he almost felt the urge to laugh, before moving in front of his mother in an effort to shield her from the sight.

For a moment Campbell, still in the throes of his sexual compulsion, turned his head back toward Easter. But then, after Montraville repeated his command to "back away," he apparently thought better of it, swore, and loosened his grip. Still, so intense was his desire for the girl, that he did not immediately let her go. "Weaver, you son of a bitch," he cried, "you do not know what you are doing. She's just a damned slave."

"Maybe so," said Montraville, "but she is *my* slave, and therefore *my* property, and you have no right to her. And in case you have forgotten, you have no right to do what you are doing, especially with a negro. Now get out of here before I go fetch a shotgun."

Campbell released Easter. She fell to the ground and commenced sobbing. For a brief moment or two, nobody moved and no one dared speak. Campbell, his eyes ablaze, stared at Montraville, who demanded: "Where is your horse, sir?"

"Next to the stable, Mr. Weaver," replied the elder, "but I need to talk to you about this. Can't we discuss it like civilized gentlemen?"

"You are not civilized, and you are certainly not a gentleman," answered Montraville. "If you are not on the horse and away from my property within two minutes I will be collecting my shotgun. There is nothing to discuss."

With that, Campbell reached down and grasped his trousers, but his initial attempt was unsuccessful. They seemed to be caught on his boots. He teetered and almost fell. And at this point John could no longer suppress his giggles. Montraville, however, was not amused.

"Easter, are you all right?"

But she clearly was not all right. She was still on the ground, whimpering with fear and trying desperately to cover her nakedness. Jane helped her to her feet and put her arms around her. Slowly they moved off to the slave quarters.

"John, go with them – make sure Easter gets back safely to the quarters and that everything is calm there. Then, Jane and John, return here. I want you to witness what I have to say to Mr. Campbell."

He then continued: "Coleman, please dress yourself, and take your time. I do not have a watch, so perhaps you will have more than two minutes. And I wish to wait for the return of John and Jane, and of course I do not want you to harm yourself, so I will make sure you return safely to your horse.

"Yes, that's good, one leg at a time." But it did seem an eternity before Campbell, shaking, was able to collect his wits and dress himself. And another eternity while the pair stood there and stared at one another with mutual loathing, before John and Jane returned.

"All right, now we can go. But I want my son and my wife to hear these words. Although I am not sure why I am saying this, because you have been warned before and you have disregarded my words, but you are never to come around here again. Further, while I have always had a certain respect for you as a preacher, if not as a man, I am now convinced that your continuing to preach the word of God and officiate over the

Church would be counter to everything I believe in and would endanger the work that the good men and women of the Church are trying to do. Do you understand me? In other words, I will be taking this matter up before the Conference. That is my promise, made before my wife and son."

"Mr. Weaver," said Campbell, "I think that would be a great mistake. I've done nothing that at least three-quarters of the free men in this county, in this state, in our blessed South have done. And what do you think the chances are that you, a mere preacher, will bring down a district elder?"

"Mr. Campbell, I do not care what three-quarters of the free men in this county or this country may have done. What you have done is contrary to the law of the land and the laws of our Church. You seem driven on by the Devil. I am perfectly willing to accept the verdict of the Conference. If they believe you should remain in your position, so be it. In my opinion they will come to a different conclusion. Now, let's go. John and Jane, you heard what I said. This will be a disagreeable task, but a task that we must undertake."

With that, Montraville took Campbell's arm and led him back to the stable. No additional words were spoken by either man. After all, what more could be said? So, after climbing back on his horse, Elder Coleman Campbell, frustrated and exasperated, and quite possibly afraid that he had met his match, rode off. And as the slow, soft hoofbeats receded in the distance, Montraville returned to the house and pondered with some trepidation his next move.

13

"Forbidden in the Word of God"

The first of November in 1859 promised to be a gray day in more ways than one. Early morning fog had given way to a persistent drizzle that tempted even those rising late to roll over and go back to sleep. But that was not an option for the delegates to the annual meeting of the Holston Conference of the Methodist Episcopal Church, South. The site of the meeting, Temperance Hall in Abingdon, Virginia, had been constructed in 1833 as the Sinking Springs Presbyterian Church and then unloaded onto the Sons of Temperance several years later.

It was, in the thinking of Bishop John Early, who would be presiding over the Conference, as unlovely a (now former) church building as he had ever seen. Perhaps it would be suitable for theatrical performances, but certainly not for a meeting such as this. Why the Conference was being held in such a place was beyond him.

But then again, maybe he was just in a sour mood because of the disagreeable subject he would have to deal with during the day's session. At any rate, he was not in a good frame of mind as he surveyed the sea of preachers displayed below him, with the blackness of their robes, relieved only by their white clerical collars, corresponding to his mood.

Early had risen from a hardscrabble upbringing in the hill country of Virginia, with little formal education, to become one of the most important and respected figures in the Church. Indeed, he had been one of the men most involved in the schism over the issue of slavery that resulted in the separation of the Methodist Episcopal Church, South from the wider Church. He was a stern man, greatly admired if not loved within the clergy. Known to his peers as "Big John," with a full head of snow white hair, described as "like the blossoms of the almond tree," piercing eyes looking out from prominent bushy brows, and a severe countenance, he commanded the pulpit as few others could. If he ever smiled, he kept it to himself.

A fiery, some might even say hot-tempered, clergyman, he was devoted to the Methodist Church. Several years before he had rejected the Whig Party nomination to run for a seat in the House of Representatives, saying: "Gentlemen, I thank you but I have a commission from a Higher Power."

He was a man who did not suffer fools gladly. He would rebuke women he felt were inappropriately attired, and was known to break off his sermons midstream to berate misbehaving congregants, including the time when several young men got up and started to leave his church while he was preaching: "I will wait until the chaff blow off and then I will preach to the wheat."

His sermons were simple and direct without any of the rhetoric and display of learning that many of his brethren engaged in. He was also known to erupt into song, shout, and stomp his feet. And it worked. Countless non-believers and followers of different faiths had been called to the altar by John Early, from his circuit riding days through his years as a bishop.

However, he was starting to feel his age. Other preachers had often talked about his iron constitution and resolute will. But in truth he was now beginning to feel all of his 73 plus years on the earth, 52 as a preacher. And he sensed that after today he would feel even older.

He would have to walk a fine line on this day, and keep a cool head when surely others would not. Still and all, he could not help but hope that, this being Temperance Hall, perhaps those in attendance would be reminded of the virtues of restraint. So, while the members and officials of the Conference were busy talking over how they had spent the night before (although it was to be hoped that given their station in life there would be little to discuss) and swapping the latest gossip, he was contemplating the difficult and sure to be contentious issue that, after almost a week of deferral and anticipation, they would now have to deal with.

That issue was a complaint by the Reverend Montraville Weaver that a presiding elder, the popular preacher, Coleman Campbell, had attempted to have carnal relations with one of Weaver's slaves. This was not the type of thing that anyone wanted aired, and attempts had been made to find a way to keep it off the agenda. But Bishop Early, who himself had faced complaints about his manner, accused of being arbitrary and discourteous to preachers at the previous Conference, had finally concluded that there was no way to avoid the matter. When Question 15: "Are all the preachers blameless in their life and official administration?" was raised in the plenary session, the members would have to hear Weaver and, if he chose to speak, Campbell.

Prior to this Conference, Early had never met Weaver, ordained as a deacon more than 20 years earlier. But he knew the man had a spotless reputation and that he was universally regarded as pious and civic-minded. Moreover, he was prosperous and used his wealth to further the Church's mission. Early had also heard stories of Weaver's many acts of kindness in administering to the poor and sick in the area. This included, apparently, those of both races.

He had even heard grumbling from a certain quarter about the man's "tender heartedness" for the "darkies." Early did not give this much notice. Besides, while Early appreciated the need for slavery he personally was on the side of those who wanted the Church to take no part in it. And he had always thought that the schism in the Church had been a great tragedy.

Campbell he did know, and he had mixed feelings about the man. As a presiding elder Campbell was responsible for overseeing the work of the local churches in his district, and he had consistently carried out those duties in an exemplary fashion. Moreover, he undoubtedly had a gift for preaching. He could move attendees at camp meetings as few others could. He seemed to possess a spiritual power that was single-handedly responsible for hundreds of new members over the past several years. But Early was only too aware that there had been rumors during those same years about his relationships with some female congregants and, most concerning, young slaves.

Several years before, Campbell had been the agent for the Holston Conference Female College, and there had been talk about him taking advantage of that position to become perhaps overly friendly with certain students. But no one had ever come forward to confront or accuse him. Still, Bishop Early was strongly of the opinion that where there was smoke, there was fire. And Campbell was also pompous, arrogant, stubborn, and bloody-minded. He did not like anyone telling him what to do, and that certainly included Early, who had tried to get him to put himself on the sidelines for a bit in the hope that this whole issue would blow over. But Campbell, convinced of his standing in the Holston Conference, had flat-out refused.

He was undoubtedly banking on his position in the Church and his many friends among both members and preachers. But Montraville Weaver was also a prominent member, with many friends. And from the dais Early could see those two camps getting organized on the floor. So with some reluctance he asked the Conference Secretary, Reverend James Nelson Sevier Huffaker, if all seemed in readiness and he had nodded his assent.

"Then we had best start and get this behind us. That is the only way we can get out of this godforsaken place and back to where we belong, doing what we should be doing."

Huffaker, who was studying the agenda, again nodded his agreement, so Early called the meeting to order, which took several minutes and much gaveling due to the hullabaloo on the floor. After welcoming the delegates to the final session he turned the meeting over to Huffaker, who would plow the Conference's way through the various routine, administrative questions which remained. He felt it would be improper to talk to either Campbell or Weaver, but as he tried to leave the chamber for what he regarded as a well-deserved cup of coffee, the elder blocked his way.

"John, you are not going to let this absurdity play itself out are you? I am wholly prepared to defend myself and I am confident that I will prevail. I do not fear the verdict of this Conference. Man to man, you know as well as I do that we are after all only human. I am not married and neither is that slave. I am accused of nothing but what half the men in this room have done."

"Coleman," replied Early, "there is nothing I can do to stop this process. Question 15 has to be considered, and I have been put on notice that Reverend Weaver will raise the issue of your conduct. You are to be charged with committing a crime forbidden in the Word of God. And the Discipline of the Methodist Episcopal Church, South clearly indicates that the case shall be fully considered and determined."

"But John, in the event that Weaver prevails, just think of the effect my expulsion would have on the laity. They need me and you need me."

Looking around, the bishop could see the eyes, and no doubt the ears, of several nearby members trying to appear as if they were following the agenda being dealt with by the secretary, while they were actually straining to discover what was going on between Early and the elder. Accordingly, he pulled Campbell off to the side and told him: "The matter is settled. If Weaver wants to raise the issue, there is nothing I can do. And in fact there is nothing I want to do. Now if you will excuse me, I need a cup of coffee. And I suggest you go back to your lobbying."

Before Campbell could say another word, Early turned and headed to the kitchen, and his much desired beverage. "Please God, just a few minutes peace," he silently prayed. He felt it would be at least a couple of hours before the main event, which he knew would be unconscionable to dump on Huffaker. But he also knew that as long as he was absent from the chair, he was fair game, or rather unfair game, for anyone who wanted to bend his ear concerning Campbell or Weaver. Accordingly, after draining his cup, and visiting the privy, he reluctantly rejoined the secretary, finding that they were about to take up Question Seven: "What traveling preachers are elected and ordained deacons?"

"James," said Early, "any problems?"

"Just that nobody seems to be paying any attention except for those raising the issues," came the reply. "But on the other hand, that means we are sailing through the agenda. We might finish up before luncheon."

"Not bloody likely," answered Early. "I do believe that our repast will be a bit late, if, that is, anyone has the stomach for it after we consider Question 15. Perhaps we should have scheduled the Love Feast for today? Seeking harmony and goodwill, forgiving our enemies, loving one another and all that? No, forget I said that. Though there will be plenty of need for one after this day is over."

But Huffaker was correct as far as the routine matters were concerned. And in short order the secretary was raising Question 15. With that, all eyes seemed to turn in the direction of Montraville Weaver. And as if in response, the reverend rose to address the Conference: "Mr. President and Mr. Secretary, it is with great pain and sorrow that I must assert that there is a preacher among us who has not been blameless in his conduct and in fact has been guilty of gross immorality, specifically an attempt to have carnal communication with a colored woman. The man is Elder Coleman Campbell."

He then proceeded to relate the incidents he had witnessed between Campbell and Easter a few months earlier, adding that his wife and son had also witnessed the incidents and were prepared to testify if necessary. In conclusion he declared: "It is my fervent hope that Elder Campbell, who has been a constructive member of the Holston Conference for many years, will acknowledge that these incidents occurred and will repent, pledging that he will mend his ways. If not, he must be expelled. Otherwise I fear that our members, especially including the many converts to our Church that he has welcomed over the years, will find in these events an excuse for their own baseness and a consequent weakening of their faith."

This naturally prompted quite a stir in the assembly. The secretary found it necessary to use his gavel, and not lightly. The issue itself and the possibility that Mrs. Weaver and her son would testify, despite the fact that such had been rumored for weeks among the clergy, were generally viewed as unprecedented in the Holston Conference. But Bishop Early, taking the chair, quickly brought the meeting to order: "Thank you Reverend Weaver. Let us first hear from Elder Campbell, if he wishes to address the Conference."

"I certainly do, Mr. President," shouted Campbell. With that, a hush settled over the attendees. There was no question now about the attention of the clergymen. All eyes were on Campbell.

"My brothers, you are well aware, I hope, of the special interest I have taken in our negroes, both slave and free. It is largely through my efforts that Church membership among the negroes, and especially among the slave population, has increased substantially. I do not have the figures before me, but I am certain that conversions of our negro slaves are outpacing those of our white brethren. Unless I am very much mistaken, the conversion of our slaves has been regarded as a priority in the Church – at least theoretically and hypothetically.

"I have, however, encountered considerable resistance among many masters who tell me that their converted slaves spend too much time in worship, too much time trying to convert others, and too much time speaking the Word of the Lord among themselves. They fear that Bible study will lead to desires on the part of their slaves to learn their letters, and perhaps even efforts by our brethren to assist them in that regard. They say that their converted slaves have become all dreamy and inclined to slack off from their labors. They say that their slaves talk about being equal before the Lord and are worried that this will make them more difficult to control and that their slaves will take it into their heads that their situation is ungodly, and that they therefore should shuck off the bonds of slavery. I have even heard them say that this is a recipe for rebellion!

"Now, you know and I know that none of this is the truth. Our converted slaves, each and every one of them, are hard-working, God-fearing men, women, and children. Rebellion is the last thing on their minds. But such is the opposition I face every day of the year. It is true that I have never heard these sentiments from the lips of Mr. Weaver, but I must say that his attitude has not always been welcoming when my mission has come to his home, where I have often stopped to administer to the negroes, to teach them and prepare them for baptism.

"In fact, Mr. Weaver has done everything in his power to impede my work. In particular, there is the matter of Easter, a young, faithless slave, but one for whom I had great hopes that she could see the light. I have talked to her and prayed over her several times, and I did believe that she was beginning to have a vision of the proper way. On the night in question, she had finally agreed to be baptized. Yes, I was embracing her, we were both I think overcome with the emotion of the occasion. But it is simply untrue that I was attempting to have carnal communication with her.

"If I have erred, it is only in being overly zealous in carrying out the Church's mission. If that is a sin, then I have sinned, and as 1st John says: 'He is faithful and just to forgive us our sins and cleanse us from all unrighteousness.'

"I have tried my best, every day of my life, since I saw the light so many years ago, to always do God's work, to always do the righteous thing, to always keep in mind the needs and desires of our Church. If I am to be punished for this sin, if that is what it was, I hope all of you will also keep in mind the needs and desires of the Church. I am but a poor, solitary soul, trying to do what is best, but with all humility I assert that I have much to offer this Church. Do not turn me out. I can only repeat that, if I erred, it was with the best of intentions, and I pledge myself to be more circumspect in the future."

With that, Campbell sat down, and after a moment of stunned silence, a murmur swept over the assembly as everyone tried to digest what had been said. In particular, there was much confusion as to whether or not he had acknowledged any guilt. Bishop Early had been hoping for a more clear-cut response, but what he had was an elder who it seemed denied any wrongdoing, although he acknowledged getting carried away, while also begging forgiveness and asserting that he was too vital to the Church to receive any significant punishment.

Trying to sort the matter out he addressed Campbell: "So let us be clear, you deny engaging in immoral conduct, but you may have gotten carried away by your overzealousness and emotion? How exactly was this overzealousness manifested?"

"Mr. President, I am frankly not certain. I admit that I may have had my arms around the slave, in a joyous celebration of her commitment to God. I can see now that this was improper, and I see also that it could easily have been misinterpreted. That was my error."

"Reverend Weaver," said a still-puzzled Bishop Early, "is it possible that you and your family might have misinterpreted Elder Campbell's behavior?"

"Mr. President," replied Weaver, "with all due respect, no. Firstly, there is the fact that on the earlier occasion I mentioned in my testimony, Mr. Campbell was doing basically the same thing, although he had not gotten as far. Then too, bear in mind that I had previously made it clear in no uncertain terms that he was not welcome at my household and that he was not permitted to minister to my slaves. Furthermore, he had previously brought gifts for Easter. And while I would prefer not to have to repeat this, there is no question that the man had his trousers around his ankles, his hands were under Easter's nightdress, which was askew, he was gripping her buttocks, and his penis was exposed, erect, and aiming for Easter's private parts.

"The man may well have been overzealous, emotional, and joyous, I am thinking especially the latter, but the reason was not because Easter had agreed to be baptized. I spoke to her the next day and she said that Campbell had awakened her and told her to follow him down the lane because he had something for her, something he did not want the others to know about. Her version of the events that led up to this incident seems to be accurate in every detail. I cannot find a flaw or equivocation in her testimony. Mr. Campbell did want to give her something that he did not want the others to know about – his male member. And if my field slave Bett, who has been like a mother to Easter, had not been awakened when Campbell came for Easter, and had not warned my overseer George, who woke me, that is exactly what she would have received.

"If there is any cause to doubt what I have said, please call on my son and my wife, who will be able to verify these simple facts. It would be disagreeable for them, in particular for Jane, but this is too important a matter for there to be any doubt about Mr. Campbell's actions. As for his standing in the Church and his importance to its mission, I have no opinion. But I do wonder, leaving aside the gross immorality on display, how such a shameless liar could be retained in such a high position."

This, of course, caused another uproar among those assembled. And it was clear that Temperance Hall was now a good deal more crowded than it had been earlier. All the seats assigned to the officially attending members were occupied, and the periphery of the room was filled with many who, Bishop Early couldn't help observing, seemed to have no business in the Hall. In fact, the walls at the back could not be seen, there were so many people lining them. The bishop was uncertain how to proceed. There was no precedent for this sort of thing, no disciplinary committee to which he could assign the matter.

A few members, probably Campbell supporters, were on their feet, clamoring for recognition, wanting to speak, but Early wondered what the point of that would be. They no doubt wanted to testify to Campbell's character and good works, but what this matter unquestionably came down to was: did he do what Weaver contended? There was no option but to allow at least John Weaver to testify. But first the room had to be cleared of anyone not officially in attendance: "Thank you Reverend Weaver. Before we proceed any further, I believe I am correct in thinking that there are many folks in attendance who have no business being here. I would therefore ask those who are not delegates to this Conference or a necessary part of the administrative staff to leave at once."

This brought about a great deal of grumbling and, at first, little movement, but eventually a line of people formed at the door and slowly left the premises. This did seem to take an eternity, and it caused Bishop Early to consider the need for a sergeant-at-arms to be designated, if not for this Conference, at least in future. "That's better. Now would everyone please take a seat and quieten yourselves. Is there any objection to allowing Mr. Weaver's son to speak?" Several delegates rose but before anyone could be recognized he practically shouted over the din: "Hearing none, Mr. John Weaver has the floor."

Montraville and John exchanged a glance before young Weaver rose and began his testimony: "What my father has said is the complete truth. I saw Coleman Campbell on two occasions, those described by my father, attempting to have congress with our slave Easter. On the second occasion, it was a very near thing. When we came upon them, Mr. Campbell was pressing Easter against a tree. He had his hands under Easter's clothing and was grasping her arse. Her bush was exposed. His trousers were around his ankles and his pego was erect and heading for the slave's pussy. I regret having to use such language in this chamber, but that is the long and the short of it."

This prompted titters from the delegates, as well as cries of "Shame," some no doubt directed at Campbell, but others at John. After another minute of fierce gaveling by Early, John continued: "Had we not arrived when we did, there is absolutely no doubt that Campbell would have had his pego up Easter's pussy where he would have taken his pleasure."

Now many chuckles could be heard in the hall, but Bishop Early was not laughing. And then he heard a voice in the back cry out: "But he is blind! How could he have seen anything?"

Again the Conference was in tumult. As Early banged his gavel, he was looking at John, who was staring right back at him. When things had calmed down, John spoke, clearly and forcefully: "I still have fair vision in one eye and some in my other. And six feet away, with a lantern, I can see just fine."

Early then performed a bit of sleight of hand behind the rostrum before raising his hand. "John, can you see the gavel I am holding in my hand?"

Came the reply: "If that is a gavel, it is the strangest one I have ever seen, shaped as it is like a Bible."

Early could not help but smile. "That is all I need to hear."

And he was now wondering if there would be any benefit, after such a nicely detailed description of the incident, in calling on Mrs. Weaver. But he supposed he must. "Thank you Mr. Weaver. Now, Mrs. Weaver, I am not going to ask you to describe what you saw. Just tell us please if what you saw is that which has been described by your husband and son."

Jane Weaver, who had been seated on the periphery of the assembly, looked toward Montraville uncertainly. He motioned for her to come to his side, which she did, and briefly they clasped hands. Then she turned toward the dais and said, in a firm voice: "Yes, without question, Mr. Campbell was about to fornicate with our slave, Easter. Mr. Campbell had been coming around, making excuses about ministering to our slaves. Easter has always been a special worry to me. She is young, intelligent but ignorant, pretty for one of her race, and without parents to keep her in check. We do not separate families and if we knew where her parents were, or any siblings for that matter, we would attempt to reunite her with them. She has been on her own since she was a young child. Indeed in many respects she is still a child. And while the other slaves have tried to protect her, there is only so much they can do when a man with the stature of Mr. Campbell 'takes an interest' in her."

Now you could hear a pin drop in Temperance Hall. But without question the attendees were favorably impressed by Jane Weaver. Early could discern nods of agreement throughout the assembly. And, truth to tell, he would have been nodding himself if he did not occupy the position he, unfortunately, did. He noted that there were a few members congregating around Campbell and talking with him, and gesticulating. Early wondered: were they urging him to speak again, to defend himself, or perhaps urging him to resign? Would we be so fortunate? After giving the situation some thought, he again addressed the group: "Thank you Mrs. Weaver. Now, Mr. Campbell, do you have anything further you would like to say?"

"Mr. President, it is sad that I must say this, but the fact of the matter is that the testimony we have heard today from the Weavers grossly misrepresents what occurred. Reverend Weaver has always borne a grudge against me, for what reason I cannot say. And naturally his son and wife would stand by him in this matter. I would also note that his son, John, notwithstanding the charade you and he just engaged in, is purblind, and his wife is, not to put too fine a point on it, a nigger-lover. I know for a fact that she is teaching some of the slaves their letters.

"As for this farcical Conference, Mr. President, I simply do not know what I have done to deserve this treatment. I have for many years sought to serve God to the best of my abilities. That has, yes, included special efforts to minister to our negro brethren. Obviously this carried some risk but I was willing to undertake it for the greater glory of God.

Mr. Weaver has consistently tried to thwart those efforts with regard to his slaves. I know not why. If the spirit of the Lord caused me to go too far in these efforts, I humbly apologize. But I can assure you that Montraville, John, and Jane Weaver have distorted my encounters with the slave Easter, either out of personal malice or jealousy with regard to my successes in the ministry. I can only await the judgment of this assembly."

At this point, Early had heard just about enough. "Mr. Campbell, there has been no charade, and if this Conference has been farcical, it is your behavior that has made it so."

Was this Early being Early? Had he gone too far, restraint never having been his strong suit? Regardless, he was pleased when one of the oldest and most respected preachers in attendance, the Assistant Secretary, Grinsfield Taylor, rose and shouted through the din: "Mr. President, this is as serious a matter as has ever been put before the Holston Conference. We are considering the expulsion of an elder of the Church, one of our most eloquent preachers, a man who has given his life over to the furtherance of our mission. I am not in a position to know exactly what went on between him and this slave of Reverend Weaver's. I believe it is perfectly possible, indeed highly probable, that Elder Campbell went beyond the bounds of propriety, but he would certainly not be the only man of God to embark on such a misstep. I urge you, and every member of this body, to consider carefully what you are about to do. And please keep in mind John 8:7."

"Thank you Reverend Taylor," replied Early, "for putting this matter into context. Indeed we must all consider carefully what is being contemplated here today in the light of our own conduct. On the other hand, even if we were to ignore or make allowances for or forgive what I personally regard as the proven immorality and baseness of Mr. Campbell, I find it impossible to condone the fact that he continues to excuse his behavior. I do not for one minute question the facts laid out by the Weaver family. I know it cannot have been easy for Reverend

Weaver to bring this matter to the Conference's attention. His testimony and that of his son and his wife have been straightforward and consistent. And yet, Elder Campbell continues to deny, obfuscate, and what's more slander his accusers.

"Let me say that while I know that Reverend Weaver's son has poor vision, I also know that if he is a few feet away from someone he can readily identify him and describe his conduct. In addition to what Mr. Campbell described as our 'charade,' John demonstrated that to me earlier today when he greeted me as we approached the Hall. And Elder Campbell's remarks with regard to Mrs. Weaver are beneath contempt.

"Further, as you know, the interests of the colored race have always been one of my principal concerns. One of my first duties involved ministering to the slaves of that great Virginian Thomas Jefferson at Poplar Forest. I managed to accomplish that mission without, as Mr. Campbell put it, becoming 'overly zealous.'

"Mr. Taylor, given all those circumstances, I cannot see my way to asking this Conference to in any way condone, or forgive, the conduct of Mr. Campbell. But that I will leave up to the delegates."

At this point, Early noted that his stomach was growling, and he realized that they had run over the time set aside for luncheon. And despite the keen interest in concluding the Campbell matter, he could see members drifting away, no doubt also feeling the need for a repast. He would have dearly loved to have decided this issue without giving the more passionate delegates favoring the position of one side or the other an opportunity to lobby those who might still be undecided. But that was clearly not going to be possible. Accordingly, he turned to Secretary Huffaker and asked him to adjourn the proceedings until after lunch, thinking that perhaps he could avoid any confrontations and, even more important, get a bit of a head start for the food.

This seemingly excellent plan however quickly fell apart when Campbell button-holed him as he stepped from the dais. "You can put a stop to this John, you know you can," said Campbell in a voice that would easily carry throughout the room. "You have the authority to discipline me if you so choose. The Conference will go along with whatever you decide. Give me a reprimand! Maybe I deserve that! But I cannot believe that it is God's plan that I be expelled."

"Reverend Campbell, you do try my patience. I am a servant of this assembly, not its dictator. And this is not something that I wish to be discussing with you at this time." With that he strode off, leaving Campbell standing by himself. He did not necessarily think anything at the time of the fact that Campbell was alone, but upon reflection later that afternoon, after the dust had settled, he should have realized that while Campbell perhaps had not given up, it appeared that his friends had.

And if Early had chanced to turn around to look at Campbell at that moment, he would have seen a picture of dejection. But he would have been happy that he did not turn around, because Early was not a cruel man, and while he did not much like Campbell, he did have a certain respect for him. And he knew that what Reverend Taylor had said earlier was true. And that if indeed Campbell were to be expelled, it would be because he had been caught with his hand in the cookie jar, not because he was the only Man of God to help himself to those cookies.

In spite of the problems confronting him, the bishop had a healthy appetite and managed to enjoy a hearty meal with a minimum of interruption. Campbell stayed well away from him, as did his friends, if indeed he still had any. But all too quickly he found himself headed back to the dais to preside over the remainder of the business session.

After the secretary called the meeting to order, Bishop Early got on with perhaps the most distasteful task he had ever had to perform as a Church official. "I believe we have heard enough about this matter from both sides. However, I do not want to stifle anyone who has anything useful to say."

He could not believe his eyes or ears – no one wanted to speak. And what's more Campbell was sitting by himself, in the back row! "Does anyone wish to propose a resolution with regard to Question 15?" One man rose, and Early was pleased to see that it was John Montgomery McTeer, like Campbell a presiding elder, and one of the most respected men in the Church. "Mr. McTeer is recognized," announced the bishop.

"My fellow members, I think you all know that this is a most unhappy duty that all of us perform today: considering the expulsion of one of us from the Church. I believe that we are all in agreement with regard to the facts. And I feel there is a growing consensus that we have no choice. The conduct engaged in by Elder Campbell, and I do not believe any of us are in any doubt about what that conduct was, cannot be tolerated in a member of the Church, let alone a high official. It must be condemned in the strongest terms. Accordingly, I move that Presiding Elder Campbell be expelled from the Church and his ordination parchment be returned to the Conference because he engaged in grossly immoral conduct, specifically attempting to have carnal communication with a colored woman."

Now the hall was virtually silent. The bishop could have whispered: "Is there a second?" But in response to his firmly voiced question several affirmative responses were heard. He then asked for a show of hands on the motion and given the virtual unanimity there was no necessity to ask if anyone was opposed. To thunderous silence, Coleman Campbell, no longer Presiding Elder Coleman Campbell, strode defiantly from the chamber, without anyone trying to stop him or follow him, and he was never to be seen in those parts again.

There were still additional routine matters to attend to before the meeting could be adjourned. These were dispensed with quickly. Slowly and calmly, the delegates bid their farewells and exited the Hall. Three or four stopped to have a few words with Montraville and shake his hand, but most wanted nothing further to do with the Campbell matter.

Coleman Campbell later appealed the expulsion and was restored to the Church and the ministry by the 1866 Holston Conference meeting because during the War Between the States records had been lost and a new hearing was impossible. He moved from circuit to circuit for a few years, but eventually had to resign when rumors about his moral character again were circulated. He continued to preach independently, but his eloquence and spiritual power had deserted him, and he died a broken man.

Easter was baptized in 1860.

14

"To Fight for the Cause"

"What did your cousin say about Zeb's disinclination to have the state secede?" Montraville asked Jane after she had returned from a visit to Mira.

"She was disinclined to talk about it. Still, I got the impression that none of the Vances has the least interest in supporting secession. Robert may be the strongest Unionist, but Zeb isn't far behind. They all think that disunion would mean war. And they know that war would mean devastation regardless of whoever wins."

And Zebulon's opinion mattered more than most, because he was a Congressman and had to be aware of what the thinking was back in Washington. And his Unionist stance seemed to be holding sway.

To Montraville's mind, that fit with what he had been hearing from his neighbors and what he himself believed. Even the slaveholders, including himself and the Vance family, had no interest in secession. In the Presidential election they had all supported John Bell, who had argued that secession was unnecessary since the Constitution protected slavery, an argument that most Western North Carolinians found compelling.

And the protection of slavery was viewed as essential, even existential, for life and prosperity in the mountain regions of North Carolina. In 1860, even though only about 10% of the population were slaveholders, there were nearly 2,000 slaves in Buncombe County alone. They worked on farms of course, but also in stands and taverns, and as laborers, clerks, and servants to professional people.

In any case, Montraville did not want to contemplate how he would be able to manage his continually expanding landholdings, now more than 3,200 acres, without his 18 slaves. And he knew that, whatever the outcome, war would change everything, and that included his family, with two sons sure to join the fight.

Things were going well and he reasoned that there was no way Lincoln would precipitate a war. But then, shortly before Christmas in 1860, the leading figures in South Carolina met in convention and unanimously adopted an "Ordinance of Secession" and a "Declaration of the Immediate Causes Which Induce and Justify the Secession of South Carolina from the Federal Union," listing what they considered violations of the rights of the Southern states, which all happened to center on the issue of slavery.

Despite that, and the secession of several other states, the call for a secession convention in North Carolina was defeated in February 1861 by 650 votes. Still, Tom Clingman and a bunch of others had not given up, calling on the legislature to reconvene.

Then came the April 12 firing on Fort Sumter, and Lincoln's call on April 15 for a militia of 75,000 men, including two regiments totaling 1,560 men to be detached from the militia of North Carolina, to put down the rebellion.

Zebulon Vance had been passionately arguing for preservation of the Union and peace. But then, in his own words:

> I was addressing a large and excited crowd, and literally had my arm extended upward... when the telegraphic news was announced of the firing on Fort Sumter and [the] President's call for seventy-five thousand volunteers. When my hand came down from that impassioned gesticulation, it fell, slowly and sadly, by the side of a secessionist.

He was not alone. There was now a rush to secession. Governor John Willis Ellis immediately rejected Lincoln's call for troops and on April

17 issued a proclamation demanding a special session of the Legislature on May 1. He also ordered seizure of all Federal property and asked for the enrollment of thirty thousand troops to be held in readiness, able to set out at one day's notice.

And the effect on the Weaver family was swift and disquieting.

"Mont, are you going to talk with Will?" asked Jane.

"As soon as he gets here, but I believe that his mind is already made up. I don't think that anything can keep him at Emory and Henry while his state is at war. You remember his frame of mind when he visited last month. The only question is, will he bother to stop off here or go directly to see Robert? I think the latter. Then my understanding is that they will be training at Camp Patton."

"He's too young, Mont," cried Jane.

"He's nearly 19, and headstrong. You know full well that I would have no influence with him. I'm even afraid to try to see Robert. If Will were to find out, he might never forgive me. No, we simply have to let him go, if that is his choice."

"And you know Fulton will go too. He's talked about serving with Zeb, if Zeb forms a company."

"There's no doubt that Zeb will be forming a company, and even less doubt that Fulton will be joining him," replied Montraville. "He's not yet married, doesn't even have his eye on anyone as far as I know. We can perhaps console ourselves with the fact that if it does happen, both Will and Fulton will be serving under the best men the South has to offer. And I suppose we can also be thankful that John cannot join them. I never thought I would feel grateful for his condition."

The partially blind John would not be allowed to serve in uniform. He had only once fired a rifle, on a hunting trip with his father, and it had not gone well, although he did manage to bag a tree.

"John will do his bit here by keeping watch over the slaves, who seem to adore him due to his condition, and making sure that the farm can provide as much food as possible for our forces. Anyhow, I fear there is no turning back now. We will all have to do whatever we can for our state and the Confederacy."

As it happens, John did try to enlist, not telling his father or mother, but the recruiters turned him down flat. One was heard to remark as John was making his way out of the courthouse that it would be more likely that he would shoot one of his fellow Rebs than any Yankee. At any rate, he would make a contribution to the cause by taking a more active role in helping around the farm.

And with perhaps more alacrity than Montraville and Jane could have imagined, even before the convention called by the legislature voted to repeal the state's ratification of the Federal Constitution and secede from the Union, Zebulon Vance was organizing his Rough and Ready Guards, the Fourth North Carolina Volunteer Infantry Regiment. And James C. Fulton Weaver was there, having left his home and business to become a private in defense of his beloved state.

The celebration that early May morning in 1861 was everything you would expect for an occasion of local boys and men heading off to glorious victory over a treacherous foe. Huge crowds had gathered. There was as yet no state flag, so people were waving all manner of banners and guidons. "Dixie" was played and sung over and over again, as tears of joy streamed down the faces of the onlookers. Jane was crying, but they weren't tears of joy.

"Mont, will we ever see him again?"

"If God wills it. Fulton is in His hands. And in Zeb's hands of course, and Fulton could not ask for a better leader. But while the Cause may be just, I fear that many of the folks who are celebrating today will look back on this as a calamitous mistake."

The marchers were all smiles as they moved down Main Street and they seemed to be in no hurry to escape the town. But soon enough they had reached the Swannanoa River where they turned east and were on their own, to whatever destiny had in mind for them. The day was fine, the route as lovely as one could wish. The men felt themselves part of a great adventure, brothers-in-arms, ready to face the battles that would come their way. And as they made camp for the night near Haw Creek, no one had any doubts. They could not, would not, fail.

Did that change for any of them during the night, the first night away from home, away from their loved ones? Did they set off the following day in a different frame of mind? Passing the Alexander Inn, which was the farthest away from home that many of them had ever been, and heading now to board a train east of Morganton for parts unknown, did any man regret his decision to fight for the cause? The answer to these questions would forever remain between each man and his Maker.

Several days later, after a stop in Statesville to collect uniforms, the regiment finally reached its training ground at Camp Hill, near Garysburg, and became Company F of the 14th North Carolina Infantry Regiment. Training was interrupted by a move to southeastern Virginia to counter a large Union force which had landed in the area, although there was to be no action for the 14th. Captain Zebulon Vance was promoted and transferred. At least he would see some action, at New Bern and in what became known as the Seven Days Battles near Richmond, before being elected Governor. For the rest of the men who had so joyously departed from Asheville, there would be a quiet summer and fall of instruction and exercises, interrupted by an August relocation to a site in Isle of Wight County. This became known as Fort Bee, in honor of General Bernard Bee, who had been killed at the Battle of Manassas in July.

The men couldn't help but feel that the year had been wasted. After General Stonewall Jackson's great victory at Manassas, the men expressed fears that the war would be over before they saw any action. Expectations were high that the South would prevail in short order. But instead, it seemed that nothing was happening. There were plenty of the old army mainstays, drilling and inspections, to keep the men occupied. But then it was just a matter of hunkering down for the winter, including the construction of log barracks where the men could while away the hours with endless card games.

By the spring of 1862, Fulton Weaver was a member of an artillery unit, the Buncombe Artillery. The local paper had this to say about the newly elected lieutenant, who had yet to see any action: he "will do to 'tie to' in any emergency." Then word came down that the Yankees were on the move. Major General George B. McClellan and his Army of the Potomac had sailed down Chesapeake Bay and were now preparing to head up the Virginia Peninsula toward Richmond. After briefly establishing itself in a defensive position near Yorktown, the 14th and the rest of General James Longstreet's forces fell back to make a stand, first at Williamsburg, and then at Seven Pines, along the Chickahominy River.

At the Battle of Seven Pines, the fighting was fierce and chaotic, and notably mismanaged by the Southern commanders, Generals Joseph E. Johnston and G. W. Smith. The result was a stalemate, with heavy casualties on both sides. Johnston was wounded and replaced by General Robert E. Lee. There was a respite for three weeks as Lee set about extending his defensive lines along the river before the Seven Days Battles. But even without bullets flying, death stalked the soldiers. For the river was surrounded by pestilential swamps. And countless troops were stricken with the disease that came to be known as the Chickahominy Fever, an affliction that may have claimed even more Southern lives during that period than combat.

Eventually, with Lee in command of the Army of Northern Virginia, the Confederates began a new offensive that was to prove successful. But Lieutenant James C. Fulton Weaver was not to have a role in it. On June 18, wracked by chills and fever, he was taken to the Chimborazo Hospital on the east side of Richmond. Thirty-eight year old Dr. James

B. McCaw had made the hospital into the largest and some would say best medical facility in the South. A dynamic, skilled, innovative, detail-oriented physician, he believed in the recuperative powers of fresh air and achieved a lower mortality rate than other large hospitals north or south.

"Nurse, do we know how long this man has had the fever?" Dr. McCaw asked as he passed by Fulton Weaver's bed.

"No sir, he was just brought in and the bearers left immediately to bring in more soldiers. I did hear one of them say that he was the worst afflicted."

"I do hope that is the case, because his chances are exceedingly remote. If he had only been brought in sooner....but you know these men don't want to admit they are sick, they don't want their comrades to think they are shirkers. We have seen hundreds of men with this condition, but I am surprised we do not see more. They practically live in the swamp, are chronically exhausted, don't get proper rest, don't get proper food, drink water contaminated with feces and the products of decaying corpses....it is a miracle they all don't come down with it."

In fact, the condition, later also called American Camp Fever by the Surgeon General's Office, was something that in many cases was impossible to treat successfully. Its symptoms, aside from chills and fever, included headache, thirst, diarrhea, bleeding from the nose, and thickening and furriness of the tongue, all due to waterborne bacteria which caused expansion and ulceration of the glands in the lining of the stomach. Sufferers found sleep difficult or impossible and were frequently delirious.

Cures, when they were attained, could take weeks or months while patients alternated between periods of remission and relapse. But even with the best care then available, and a dedicated staff of doctors and nurses, many of those who suffered the fever, including Fulton Weaver, could not be helped. On the 20th, at a little after noon, he vomited up a substance with the appearance of coffee grounds and died peacefully and calmly.

His parents received the dreadful news in a letter from Fulton's commanding officer:

Camp 14th N.C. Troops near Richmond Va.
June 21st,
REV. M. M. WEAVER

Dear Sir,
It becomes my painful duty this morning to communicate to you the sad intelligence of   the death of your beloved son J. C. F. Weaver — Fulton has been suffering severely with chills for a long time as perhaps you know — last Tuesday when we were ordered to come to this camp I went to Fulton then still with us and told him that he should not go with the Co. except against my orders for I saw he was very sick. I had him sent to Chimborazo Hospital Richmond where he died June 20 — His death is the first intelligence I recd. after he left his Co.

J.M. Whitmire and A.G. Haren of my Co. are convalescents in the same hospital and will see that he is decently interred. To remove him now is impossible — no corpse is permitted to pass over the same owing to pressure of business saluting the Army. You & family alone feel more keenly this bereavement than I do — A shadow is now cast over the entire Co. by whom he was much loved.

In friendship, sympathy, & bereavement,
your humble servt.
D. M. GUDGER
Capt. Co. "F" 14th N.C.T.

Montraville hastened to Richmond and was successful in collecting his son's remains. Since the railroads and stagecoaches would often refuse to transport bodies in ordinary wooden caskets, Fulton Weaver made the return journey to Reems Creek in a box containing a casket which had been sealed tight by wrapping it in a large piece of osnaburg fabric that had been dipped in boiling tar.

He arrived home barely a year from when he and his comrades had set out with so much joy and optimism. At his funeral, a large crowd of weeping family, neighbors, and friends were out in force to pay tribute to the young man who, as the *Asheville News* reported, "laid down his life on his country's altar."

Understandably there was nary a dry eye in the church as the preacher delivered his eulogy:

> The ravages of war furnish an additional cause of grief in the death of yet another noble young man of the mountains. We are here to mourn and celebrate the life of J C F Weaver, called Fulton by all those who knew and loved him. From childhood he was more than ordinarily sedate and thoughtful. As he grew up he became confirmed in habits of industry, sobriety and unremitting attention to business, which gave cheering promise of future success. He had already gathered around him a comfortable property and, established in a good time, he had commenced business for himself. When the present unnatural war — provoked by the fanaticism of our enemies and sustained by the lust for power and plunder for which they are noted — assumed threatening proportions, Mr. Weaver, in the manhood of his strength, with many other gallant sons of the mountains, organized that noble company, the Rough and Ready Guards, under the leadership of the intrepid Vance, threw themselves into the breach between the

invaders and the loved ones at home. They marched from Asheville the 3rd of May, 1861, little more than two weeks after that unscrupulous, outlaw-politician Abraham Lincoln had the unimaginable effrontery to request troops to descend upon this great, peace-loving state — the second company from the Volunteer county. From that time to the day of his death he was engaged, with his company, in defending the coast of his own state and Virginia.

In his proper place amidst his comrades in arms, Mr. Weaver fought valiantly at the Battle of Williamsburg. He was also among the daring spirits of the "Seven Pines," and in these actions, most nobly no doubt, did he and his company sustain the high renown of his own "Old North State." For a considerable time he had been chilling, but still was able to do his whole duty as a soldier up to the 18th of this month, when he was removed from camp to the Chimborazo Hospital in Richmond, Virginia. On the evening of the same day he was taken violently ill, perhaps with congestive chill, and on 20th June, a little after 12 o'clock noon, he departed peacefully and calmly as the sleeping of an infant.

Mr. Weaver had been for some years a member of the Methodist Episcopal Church, South, and a professor of the religion of our common savior, and it is said by one of his company whose letter is now before me, that he never engaged in the dissipations too common in camps, but while others were engaged in gaming and the like, Fulton employed many of his leisure hours in reading the Bible a mother's hand had placed in his as the last and best token of her affection. Thus has passed away one of nature's true noblemen — an honest man — one who loved his friends, his home, his country, and in defense of which he has offered up his life. Now will sleep in his family burying ground the young soldier and Christian till called to the better home above. Though his death is a great calamity to his kindred and friends, and especially afflictive to a fond mother and affectionate sisters, yet, even in this sad bereavement, they have this consoling fact left them, that he demeaned himself well in all the relations of life, and fell nobly in the van of his country's defenders.

In the noble and immortal words of the great Scottish poet Thomas Campbell, in his stanzas to the memory of the Spanish patriots killed resisting the despots of their time:

> Glory to them that die in such a cause!
> Kings, Bigots, can inflict no brand of shame,
> Or shape of death, to shroud them from applause:
> No! — manglers of the martyr's earthly frame!
> Your hangman fingers cannot touch his fame!'

"So sorry, Jane, Mont, he was a fine man. Our cause may be just, but I fear victory will come at a cost that we will not want to pay," said Jacob Weaver, as he embraced a tearful Jane and a stoical Montraville.

"Thank you Jacob. We both know that he was never one to neglect his duties as he saw them. I assume you saw the death notice in the *News*? 'Faced the foe and assisted to repulse them from the bloody field,' and 'hurled death into the face of the insolent invaders.' Cold comfort indeed. If only I could remember him like that. But in my nightmares all I see is a miserable, frightened young man thrashing about in a hospital bed, waiting to breathe his last. And what I fear is that he will not be the last from the family to lose his life to this struggle."

"I of course have the same fear. There can be little doubt now that this accursed war will not be easily or quickly won."

"How is your son James Thomas faring? I understand he's in McDowell's Battalion?"

"Yes, he is. The unit was mustered in weeks ago, but they are still awaiting word of where they are to report," replied Jacob. "The good news, perhaps, is that he has been elected a junior second lieutenant. Have you heard from Will? I understand he is with the 29th?"

"We have received a couple of letters. He is their color sergeant and is somewhere in Tennessee, or maybe Kentucky. The unit was in action near the Cumberland Gap in March, fighting off the Yankees trying to take some fort there. He said that Col. Vance climbed up on top of a mountain and with his field glasses spotted the flash of a bayonet in the distance. It was the enemy trying to catch them unawares. I'm not sure from the letter whether Will even fired his rifle, but it seems that the enemy withdrew.

"His most recent letter, received just a few days ago, makes it seem like not much is going on, which I doubt. But if he is being truthful, we are thankful for that. He did rail against the locals that have been caught messing about with them. Cutting down telegraph wires to interfere with their communications and such. He says there are spies everywhere. Have you heard anything from Rufus? I thought sure he would be here, and I was wondering what he is going to do."

"I haven't seen him in months. I don't get over his way often. But I can tell you one thing for sure, Rufus won't be joining up. He's a loyalist through and through, which may be why he is not here today. If he is conscripted, he will find a substitute. He wants nothing to do with the war, especially on our side."

"Neither do I, never did and certainly do not now, but it is happening and the law is the law," replied Montraville. "And surely he cannot afford a substitute?"

"Maybe not. But I do believe that Rufus will head for the hills, and possibly even to the Union forces in Tennessee, if the 'recruiters' come for him. He is no coward. But he cannot countenance disunion."

"That is what makes this conflict so very regrettable. Men, good men, the best men, who should be working together to obtain a better future for themselves, instead are killing each other because of a difference of opinion. I have no quarrel with the view that a principal is worth fighting for. But is it worth dying for? Not in my view."

To which Jane added, through her tears: "You know, Jacob, I believe that slavery must be preserved, and that Lincoln is the cause of this conflict. But if it would bring this war to an end I would free all our slaves in an instant and prostrate myself before that evil man."

To which Jacob could only reply: "Since we know that is not going to happen and that this war is likely to continue for years, we can only pray and hope that God's will is to keep our men safe."

Of course it was not. By the end of the war, North Carolina had contributed more men, and boys, to the Confederate killing machine than any other state. But William Elbert Weaver, "Will," was spared. For awhile there wasn't much going on, but on Christmas Day of 1862 his unit under Col. Robert Vance, was ordered to join up with General Braxton Bragg's army in the vicinity of Murfreesboro, Tennessee. There, the Army of Tennessee, 35,000 strong, confronted Major General William Rosecrans' Army of the Cumberland with 43,000 men. There was a savage battle, with casualties believed to be the highest, percentage-wise, on both sides, of the entire war. For three days the Confederates attacked repeatedly but were repulsed by massive Union artillery.

Legend has it that on the morning of the last day of the year the black horse of the valiant but impulsive Col. James E. Rains, exhorting his men with the cry of "Forward my brave boys, forward!," continued into the Federal lines after Rains was shot from the horse's back and killed, and then returned in the afternoon ridden by a Yankee officer who was also shot dead. This was surely the only instance in the war in which an officer from each side was killed on the same day riding the same horse. Col. Rains was replaced in command by Col. Vance, whose horse was shot out from under him but who was able to continue the battle. He would later report that Private David Patton of the Buncombe Life Guards was killed by a shell, taking off his head, which landed in the fork of a tree.

That night, it was said, was a "sleep with the dead," as the Confederate troops drowsed upon a ground strewn with piles of dead soldiers.

But luck, or God, was with Sergeant, later Captain, Weaver, who early in the war had been reported killed in action, only to turn up to the great surprise of first his commanding officer, who immediately sent him home on leave, and then his mother (and some grave-diggers). He managed to survive the Siege of Vicksburg, and the Battles of Chickamauga, Latimer House, Smyrna, and Allatoona Pass. He then saw action in the Battles of Spanish Fort and Fort Blakely, defending Mobile, where he witnessed a charge by several regiments of United States Colored Troops against the Confederates' well-fortified position. He later said, "whole brigades...were murdered right there."

Weaver and his fellow soldiers managed to hold off a force many times their size for 12 days and then slip away unseen through an alligator- and snake-infested swamp. They then marched to Enterprise, Mississippi where they joined up with troops under General Richard Taylor, who finally surrendered on May 4, 1865. Weaver departed after his parole was received and returned by way of Alabama and Georgia to western North Carolina in August. He became a lawyer, named one son Montraville, and another, who became a Congressman, Zebulon, and died at the age of 93.

Such was not to be the case with Jacob's son, Lieutenant James Thomas Weaver. After a couple of months drilling on an island in the French Broad below Warm Springs, his unit, the 60th North Carolina

Infantry Regiment, moved to the vicinity of Murfreesboro. There, for a time, all was quiet. In a letter to Will, he related a visit to his Aunt Christina, 30 miles north, finding her an even stronger secessionist after "...the Yanks took everything from her that they could make serve their purpose." He had comforts: "Having camped close to a big brick kiln, I and Corp'l Harg have a nice brick chimney to ourself, and a good fire in it, and that is very pleasant [in] this snowy weather."

But the calm was to be short-lived and at year's end he was to fight in the same battle at Murfreesboro as his cousin Will. In March of 1863, he became a captain and soon thereafter his unit was moving toward Vicksburg, part of an effort to relieve General Ulysses S. Grant's siege. They reached the banks of the Big Black River on Independence Day, only to learn that the city had surrendered, whereupon they were ordered to Jackson in an attempt to defend that capital city, which had been reoccupied after being virtually destroyed two months earlier by General William Tecumseh Sherman. Heavy fighting ensued, but in short order the city was again taken by the Union Army and the Confederates withdrew.

In September the unit was ordered to the northwest corner of Georgia to reinforce Bragg's Army of Tennessee. In what was to be the battle with the second highest casualty figures of the war after Gettysburg, the 60th distinguished itself by achieving the farthest Confederate advance. Captain Weaver became an acting lieutenant colonel when his commanding officer was severely wounded and had to leave the field of battle. Shortly thereafter he was promoted to major, owing to his "cool and gallant conduct in the late battle of Chickamauga."

At Missionary Ridge, Brigadier General Alexander Welch Reynolds hailed his "...conspicuous gallantry...an intrepidity and indifference to danger seldom surpassed."

James Thomas Weaver survived Stoney Ridge, the Johnston-Sherman Atlanta campaign, and Franklin, but on December 7, 1864, as he led his men in support of General Nathan Bedford Forrest's attacks on the enemy at, again, Murfreesboro, Weaver was picked off by a sharp-shooter and died instantly.

A fellow officer said of him: "How often when the balls were thickest and the shells shrieked the loudest have we heard his voice...'Steady boys, there's no danger!'" And another officer called him ".... as gallant a soldier, as true a man, as devoted a citizen as was ever produced in North Carolina....with a heart as true and tender, as gentle as ever was the heart of the gentlest of women."

Illustrating the push and pull of Union and Confederate sentiment in the mountains of western North Carolina, Rufus Thaddeus Weaver, the son of Montraville and Jacob's brother James, did eventually join the Federal forces, enlisted by Yankee recruiters active in the North Carolina mountains as a private. His unit was the newly formed Third Regiment of North Carolina Mounted Infantry, part of the notorious Kirk's Raiders.

George Washington Kirk was a deserter from the Confederate Army who, after switching sides, used guerilla tactics to effect a reign of terror in the eastern Tennessee and western North Carolina region. He and his men, including fellow deserters and Unionists from around Shelton Laurel, sought to undermine the Southern cause by theft, sabotage, looting, helping escaping slaves and deserters, information gathering, and, in general, wanton violence and bloodshed. Their tactics took the brutality of war to a new level. As a newspaper said at the time: "...the intention of these outlaws [was] to waste our wheat fields, in order, if possible, to starve the people into submission.... Who but savages, yes, savages, resort to such a mode of warfare? The history of the world does not contain an instance when it has been done."

The 3rd Regiment's most famous raid involved a movement, without being detected by Confederate forces, from Knoxville, Tennessee, on June 13, 1864, to Camp Vance, used for conscript training, near Morganton NC. There, on June 28, they took over the camp and destroyed railroad facilities and other structures. One hundred thirty-two men were taken prisoner, while 40 others joined the Raiders. The following day, as they were making their way back to Tennessee, they were set upon by Confederate troops, but using their prisoners as human shields they forced the Southern forces to back off.

Later, in a skirmish with the Burke County home guard at the Winding Stairs, Kirk's men mortally wounded one of the largest slave-holders in the region, William Waightstill Avery, a legend in those parts for, himself a lawyer, having shot and killed another lawyer in court. Avery had called his courtroom adversary a fraud and outside the court-room been horsewhipped by the man. When they met up a couple of weeks later, in another courtroom, the man insulted Avery before the presiding judge, whereupon Avery calmly pulled out a pistol and shot the other man through the heart from five feet away. Avery was tried a few days later and found not guilty of murder by a jury which deliberated for all of ten minutes. They concluded that his actions had been caused by extreme provocation which led to temporary insanity.

He was the last of three brothers killed in the war, the most well known being Colonel Isaac E. Avery who, unable to speak after being mortally wounded at Gettysburg, scrawled a note for his father using his own blood: "... tell my father I died with my face to the enemy."

In October 1863 Kirk's men had killed another prominent slave-holder, John Woods Woodfin, son of the former Buncombe County clerk of court, in a skirmish near Warm Springs. Major Woodfin's cavalry battalion had attacked Kirk's regiment, which had settled into the Warm Springs Hotel after overrunning a nearby detachment of Confederate in-fantry. Although they succeeded in expelling the raiders from the area, Woodfin was shot from his horse by one of Kirk's marksmen, firing from the hotel balcony as the Major was crossing the French Broad River. Aside from the loss of Major Woodfin, the engagement was significant and possibly unique inasmuch as it pitted a regiment of mostly Southern

Unionists against a regiment of local Southern Confederates on what was essentially their home turf.

In February 1865, Kirk attacked Waynesville, stealing everything in sight, including horses, killing a dozen or so men, freeing prisoners from the jail, and burning down several houses, including the homestead of War of Independence hero Colonel Robert Love.

The 3rd Regiment in April and May of 1865 patrolled in the area north of Asheville and then took part in the occupation of the city. Rufus Weaver survived the war but during it became consumptive. He moved shortly thereafter to Blue Ridge Township near Hendersonville, where he died, aged 47.

So Rufus would probably not have been counted among the 31,000 to 40,000 North Carolina soldiers who died in the war, or the 620,000 to 750,000 American soldiers who died in the war: around 2.5% of the U. S. population. The equivalent today would be around 7 million deaths. These are staggering numbers which leave aside the estimated 60,000 who survived but lost limbs. Or the 50,000 or so non-combatants who died. And there are those who feel these numbers are an undercount. Nobody really knows. It may have been necessary, it may have been unavoidable. But perhaps, as Benjamin Franklin said: "There was never a good war, or a bad peace." Although if Franklin had experienced the immediate aftermath of this war he might not have been so sure there was never a "bad peace."

15

"On the Home Front"

It must be said that Buncombe County suffered relatively little during the war, aside of course from the many men who never returned or who returned grievously wounded in body and/or spirit. There were occasional raids by bushwhackers and Kirk's ragtag forces. And the Weavers were not immune. Several years before, Montraville had swapped some of his land on Flat Creek for his cousin Joseph Eller's land on the Dry Ridge that was to become downtown Weaverville, and had built a new home for his family, the first house in town. On the evening of April 3, 1864, a Sunday of all days, Montraville heard a group of horses approaching.

"Jane, where is John? I think we may have some unwanted guests."

"I think he is with Eliza. Who do you think it is?"

"Could be raiders. I'll deal with 'em. Find John and the young'uns and take 'em into our bedroom."

There were indeed a dozen or so horsemen approaching the house. Montraville went outside. He couldn't see any uniforms, which didn't necessarily mean anything if they were raiders.

As they pulled up in front of him he asked the rider in the lead, who was presumably in charge: "What is your business here?"

"We don't want no trouble; all we want are your weapons. We're from Col. Kirk's regiment up in Laurel and we've already been to some of your neighbors, and everyone has been cooperative." He turned around: "Tom, George, and Isaac, please accompany Mr. ---" Turning back he said, "Sorry, I didn't get your name."

"It is Reverend Weaver."

"I'll be damned! You're the second Reverend Weaver tonight. Is he your brother?"

"Presumably. He lives nearby. Listen, my wife and children, including a blind boy, are inside."

"Don't worry. We are going to make this quick. I suspect your forces have already been alerted, and we have no interest in your family. My men will accompany you while you go back inside and show us what you have. And don't try to hide anything. All we want are firearms and swords. And ammunition of course." Then he motioned for a couple of others to look in the barn and the other outbuildings.

Montraville, already striding back into the house, answered: "There are no swords. And only a couple of rifles we use for hunting." He had already decided to cooperate, and he thought it most unlikely that they would turn up the better arms hidden under the flooring.

"You won't be using 'em for huntin' anymore. We'll be using 'em for killin' Rebs."

While the leader and the rest of his men waited nervously outside, Montraville watched as the three raiders combed through the house, briefly looking into the bedroom where Jane was trying her best to keep calm and set a good example for her children. She wondered if Montraville would indeed hand over their weapons. She was hoping so.

Then suddenly, down the road more horses could be heard, their riders urging them on. And the three raiders hightailed it outside carrying a couple of rifles which frankly weren't in great shape and not much of a loss. The others were already on the move. The three mounted their horses and headed off after them. A couple of minutes later, a small detachment of Confederate cavalry appeared, the officer yelling at Montraville, who was unnecessarily pointing toward the retreating raiders, "We'll get 'em."

But Montraville doubted it. As Jane came to his side, he said: "They won't catch them. The raiders know the territory better than they do, and I'll warrant have better mounts. And I'm figuring there were no out-rages at the other homes. So vengeance is not required. We will certainly read in the *News* that the enemy made their escape. At any rate, we are safe, that is the only important thing. However, I am glad they didn't get what we hid under the floorboards."

"You took a chance there, didn't you? What if they had had more time and had found the Whitworths?"

"They seemed to be happy with the old Springfield and the Enfield, and a little powder. The Whitworths are so well-hidden they'd have never found them. You weren't worried were you?"

To which Jane could only nod, and put her arms around her hus-band and her head against his chest, in a vain attempt to hide her tears.

The ongoing possibility of these sorts of raids in the area meant that everyone had to be constantly on guard. And they would have certainly been frightening for the inhabitants. Nevertheless, in truth, on the home front there was no significant military activity until the so-called Battle of Ashe-ville on April 6, 1865, three days before Lee's surrender at Appomattox.

The town of 1,200 might have been considered a promising target, since at one time it held a rifle factory, although the equipment had been removed and taken elsewhere. In fact, why it had been spared for so long seems a mystery. At any rate, when word got out that Union forces were marching on the city, Col. George Wesley Clayton assembled a "force" to take them on. This outfit was comprised of home guards, convalescent soldiers, and anyone else that could be strong-armed into joining the fight, including the "Silver Grays," which counted among its members a 14-year-old boy and a 60-year-old Baptist minister. By the afternoon they had set up a defensive position on a hillside near the French Broad River, overlooking the route on which the Union forces were advancing.

Colonel Isaac M. Kirby, in command of the Union forces, may have perceived that the enemy was stronger than it was or may have concluded that being as the war was clearly almost over, close combat was not desirable.

At any rate, there were few casualties, and the Yankees retreated after an exchange of sporadic long-range cannon and rifle fire that lasted several hours.

They left in a hurry, discarding weapons and equipment along the way, and did not return.

Buncombe County was spared incidents such as the Shelton Laurel massacre in Madison County, more of a Unionist stronghold. There a gang of Unionists and Confederate deserters, desperate for food and the salt necessary to preserve food during the winter, had raided Marshall and terrorized the family of Col. Lawrence Allen, Commander of the 64th North Carolina Regiment. Upon hearing of this, Allen and Lt. Col. James Keith sought revenge, marching with their forces on Shelton Laurel where they tortured women to tell where their men were hiding, torched and knocked down homes, slaughtered livestock, and eventually executed twelve men and a thirteen-year-old boy without trial. Few, if any, of those executed had had anything to do with the original raid.

The most excitement in Buncombe County until the waning days of the war may have been the incident of the bear. In 1863 a pair of Tennessee brothers, sentenced to be hanged as Union sympathizers, escaped to North Carolina and hid in caves in the Reems Creek gorge. They were apparently living comfortably there, foraging and hunting for squirrels and rabbits, when one day they returned from a fishing expedition to find that a couple of bears had taken up residence in the cave. Fortunately for the brothers, they were either able to make friends with the bears or find shelter elsewhere.

But word had gotten out that the brothers were hiding in the cave. So a posse of local residents was formed and one of its members fired a shot at the supposed hiding place, which resulted in the bears exiting the cave and heading for the locals, who turned and ran, never to return. One of the men allegedly reported that "them blasted Yankees have done gone and drafted bears to do their fightin' for 'em."

Asheville actually prospered during the war, since it was stable and had been spared major military activity. There was, for a time, the rifle factory and a distillery to make whiskey for Confederate Army hospitals. Slavery continued to be profitable, and expanded, with slaves even working in the rifle factory making weapons for the army. Fees for slaves increased, doubling every year and then some.

But that all changed by the war's end. Two weeks after the Battle of Asheville, Union troops led by General George Stoneman, but under the command of General Alvan Cullem Gillem, approached the city and negotiated a truce with the local Confederate forces under Brigadier General James Green Martin, a resident of Asheville. Gillem had been notified of Confederate General Joseph E. Johnston's surrender to General Sherman, and with Lee's surrender two weeks earlier at Appomattox it seemed the war was effectively over.

The truce allowed the Union soldiers to march unchallenged through Asheville and obtain some food supplies and forage for their horses. In return, Gillem promised there would be no violence or destruction and that he would return his forces to Tennessee. On April 24, the men in blue passed quietly through Asheville, some of the residents waving from their porches.

However, a few days before, unbeknownst to Gillem, President Andrew Johnson had rejected the peace terms and ordered Sherman "to push his military advantages." After making camp several miles north of Asheville, Gillem, desirous of pursuing a career in politics, turned the command over to General Simeon Brown and made haste toward Nashville, Tennessee. Brown then ordered two of his brigades to return to Asheville. The Union forces, no doubt unhappy about the turn of events (they had been on the march for weeks and thought they were headed home) and angry about the assassination of President Abraham Lincoln, only then becoming widely understood, pillaged the town between April 26th and 28th. They broke into homes, ransacked them, stole food and anything else of value, burned public buildings, and took judges and other officials prisoner.

Hundreds of men and boys were rounded up and crammed into two warehouses. General Martin, a hero of the Mexican War, in which he had lost his right arm, was luckier than most. He was quickly released under a flag of truce. But then, arriving at his home, he found "Mrs. Martin and my daughters going over the house with a squad of Federal soldiers holding candles for them to examine all the trunks and for such things as they fancied for themselves."

Captured prisoners, officials, and even prominent citizens, including Reverend Branch Merrimon, were marched out of town to the west. Sometime later newly promoted General William J. Palmer released the officials and apologized, but the damage had been done. Asheville had suffered what General Martin called the worst plundering he had heard of in the war.

When the blue-clad forces marched out for good on April 28, they were followed by a procession of hundreds of freed slaves. Some had "requisitioned" their former owners' property, including horses and carriages. There was much singing and laughter. One woman, astride a scruffy old nag, her few possessions piled beneath her, shouted: "Glory, glory! We's free, we's free. Glory hallelujah!" over and over again.

The aftermath of the war was not kind to Asheville and Buncombe County. In addition to the destruction by Brown's forces, the economy was in ruins. The currency, including Confederate bonds and money, was worthless. Of course, the "investments" in slaves had been wiped out. Many properties had been destroyed and looted. Agricultural products had largely been consumed and livestock herds decimated. The social network was in tatters. There was no credit to be had, except at ruinous interest rates, resulting in a largely barter economy and numerous bankruptcies.

Community leaders attempted to get things moving. Both Nicholas Woodfin and William Baird tried to get new factories going but failed. Crime was rampant. Land values plummeted. The Plank Road Company went out of business and other roads, including the Buncombe Turnpike, after years of neglect, were in serious disrepair. The county had to sell off part of the public square, which was at any rate only a muddy expanse occupied mostly by wild hogs and men drunk on cheap corn whiskey. There were few able-bodied men, the workforce having been depleted by death and disability. And the political system was in complete disarray.

In addition, there was lots of score-settling – it should be borne in mind that the War Between the States was also a war within those states, especially in western North Carolina and eastern Tennessee, and in that regard it had not really ended. Communities, even families, had been torn apart. People who had been driven out by their neighbors returned. Feuds erupted. And of course race relations were uneasy at best, and violent at worst.

The whites in the mountains had been just as committed to slavery as the big plantation owners. The difference in western North Carolina was that there were fewer slaves relative to the white population, and the slaveholders and the slaves themselves were more diverse. There was less corporal punishment and less family division. Treatment, conditions, and the work in general were less harsh than was the case farther south. But it was still slavery.

And many mustered-out black Union soldiers stayed in Buncombe County. A company of black soldiers had been left behind to hold Asheville; many remained when they were discharged. If they felt entitled to lord it over those they had vanquished who could blame them? Cries of "How do you like this?" and worse were directed at the citizenry. Things were further inflamed when a few members of the First U.S. Colored Heavy Artillery, garrisoned near Asheville, were suspected of raping a young white woman, found guilty in a drumhead court martial, and executed and dumped in a shallow, unmarked grave near what is now the intersection of Broadway and Mt. Clare Avenue.

As the weeks and months went by, many former slaves traveled to Asheville. They were often homeless and hungry. Whites who were not openly hostile took advantage of them. It was not uncommon for former slaves, especially those who talked politics, flaunted their independence, or tried to exercise their right to vote, to be defrauded of their wages by their employer's threats of dismissal prior to payment. Arrests for the crime of loitering were used to get them to accept bad work contracts. And they found little assistance from the Freedmen's Bureau. Lt. Patrick E. Murphy was appointed the Assistant for a multi-county area in March of 1866 and with limited funding and few resources, and poor support from Washington, did what he could, obtaining in many instances payments which white residents had withheld from black men and women who had done work for them.

But in far too many cases he was essentially powerless. And from the time that Lt. Murphy left his post in November 1866 until July 1867, when Oscar Eastmond became the Bureau's agent and again was able to assert some Federal authority, there was effectively no one in charge of the Bureau in Buncombe County. Making matters worse, the civil government was largely comprised of the same elites that had been in charge during the war. Local courts apprenticed black children to white property owners. And many white judges even refused to allow Negroes to testify in court, or went out of their way to favor whites in prosecutions involving race issues.

In 1867 three members of Asheville's Union League, a biracial organization seeking to elect Republicans to office, were assaulted and nearly killed in attacks. Then in the spring of 1868 the Ku Klux Klan arrived on the scene, urging members to hit "when darkness reigns," and local Negroes began arming themselves.

During the voting in the Presidential election later that year, a black man, James Smith, was prevented from voting by a white county clerk.

An altercation ensued in which Smith was knocked to the ground, followed by both sides taking to the streets, waving weapons and shouting at each other. Then a black man who had voted for the Democratic candidate, Horatio Seymour, was confronted by Negroes who had been battling whites throughout the morning. Whites, including the Merrimon and Patton families, came to his defense. Then Smith threw a rock at the black voter and all Hell broke loose. Shots rang out and Smith lay dead, while many other black men were injured.

The *Asheville News* reported, not entirely sympathetically: "No man deplores the occurrence more than ourself, and we believe in that we express the feelings of every white citizen of the town and if the true citizens of Asheville had had any influence with the negroes, it would not have occurred, for it was evident from the time of the first fracas, that a terrible outbreak was brewing, and if the proper authorities, or those who profess to be the only friends of the negroes, had advised them to go home after voting, the last and fatal difficulty would not have happened."

Interestingly, the former abolitionist, author of *The Impending Crisis of the South*, Hinton Rowan Helper, was now residing in Asheville and working as a land agent. From his adopted town (he could never return to the Piedmont) he ranted, in print at any rate, about the inferiority of Negroes and other minorities and the need to expel them from the United States.

Abolitionist he may have been, but now he was an unapologetic, strident white supremacist, the author of the most incendiary, racist tomes imaginable. For example, in *Nojoque, A Question for a Continent*, he argued that: "Were I to state here, frankly and categorically, the primary object of this work is to write the negro out of America and that the secondary object is to write him (and manifold millions of other black and bi-colored caitiffs, little better than himself,) out of existing, God's simple truth would be told." Reputedly, Helper would not stay in an inn or seek sustenance at an eating establishment that employed Negroes.

It is doubtful that Helper's presence exacerbated the situation, since it is said that he maintained a low profile and was "always alone." In any event the election of Republican William W. Holden as governor in 1868 convinced the Congress that reconstruction had been successfully implemented and the Freedmen's Bureau office in Buncombe County was ordered closed by the end of the year. So the situation simmered, only occasionally reaching a boiling point, thereafter.

16

"A New Order"

Montraville Weaver was better-situated to deal with the post-war reality than were most of his fellow Buncombe County residents. He was not in debt and had substantial landholdings, including much of Hamburg Mountain and land along Reems Creek above the Penland to the head of the creek. But he was very much unsure of how he was going to manage without his slaves.

He felt that he had been a just, even-handed master. He had rejected overtures from the speculators that infested the region, seeking owners who might be willing to sell excess slaves that could be turned into nice profits farther south. It must be said that this was not entirely a sign of his "benevolence," since the presence of speculators tended to stoke fear among slaves, creating problems he was not interested in dealing with.

His slaves had been given a bit of responsibility and latitude, if not freedom and independence, and had been trained as cooks, nannies, smiths, and in all kinds of farming and animal husbandry. And he believed that they appreciated his actions on behalf of Easter.

But he harbored no illusions. He understood the inescapable fact that their status as slaves and his as master rendered valueless any sense he might have of their attitude toward him. They had been his property. They no longer were.

Montraville had not been in Asheville when the town had been ransacked but he received regular reports from there, including the exodus of the former slaves. And he had been hearing rumblings from his slaves, who could not help but overhear the many discussions in his house about the situation and knew that they had been freed by President Lincoln in 1863. And now they knew that the war was over and that the Confederacy and slavery were no more. What he had long regarded as the natural order, whites meant to lead and rule, Negroes meant to be controlled and subjugated, had crumbled into dust. It was time for a reckoning.

Many ex-slaves on nearby farms had already vanished. He found out one morning that their number included two of his own, Jennie and Bett. The others, so far, remained. He hoped that at least some of them would continue to do so.

Accordingly, he gathered them together and addressed them: "There is a new order in the land. I recognize that. As long as you have been here, I have tried to be a fair master. You can judge for yourselves whether or not I succeeded."

At this point he paused and looked into the eyes of each person before him. Was it his imagination, or did he see something different in those faces, faces that he had come to know so well? They were not smiling. He had seen them smile, on those occasions when there was something to smile about. At some sort of celebration, when there was music, when the food was plentiful or when new clothes were being distributed. Even at church. Now he saw no smiles. But no fear was evident either, or even unease. And no hint of the subservience he was used to seeing, or at any rate, was used to reading in their faces. Rather, he now saw mostly calm, solemn, confident expressions. As his eyes moved from face to face, Montraville could not help feeling that each man and woman in front of him was more certain of the future, and more looking forward to the future, than he was.

"God knows it has not been an easy time. And that is a fact, God does know. And I think you will agree with me that He has watched over us. And I think you will also agree with me that we need to continue trusting in the Lord. True, we suffered the worst fate possible with Fulton's death, but we never wanted for food, and in this area we have been spared the bloody horrors and sicknesses that so many others have experienced."

Again he paused, thinking of Fulton, and the other men who had given their lives for such a foolish endeavor. Then he continued, forcing himself to carry on before he started weeping in front of those people before whom he had always been so careful to conceal any emotion.

"In any event, although I feel a sense of responsibility for you, you are no longer my property. You are free to make your own lives now. I will assist you to the extent that I can. But this land is still mine. You may stay and work for me, or see if you can find better work elsewhere, or follow the others who went trailing off after the Yankees. I've heard that there is a contraband camp near Knoxville. I cannot speak to what you may find there.

"Here there is work if you want it. At present there is no question of wages because at present there is no money. I am hopeful that the economy will right itself soon, and that I will be able to pay you for your work. You will receive a fair share of any income we earn from every harvest. But in the meantime there is food and clothing and shelter. Your quarters are yours to do with as you wish. You can keep your bed and bedding, clothes, cooking pots, tables, chests and tubs. When you are not working, you are free to come and go as you like. You can leave whenever you want. You will not be disciplined. But if anyone causes trouble, you will then be asked to leave, or in serious cases turned over to the authorities.

"You may recall that a few years ago I contracted with Mr. Peters to cultivate my land down on Flat Creek. We agreed that he could build a cabin there and grow crops of my choosing. I supplied the seed and tools, and animals when necessary, in exchange for a portion of the crop he would give me. You men have always done a good day's work for me. That could be an opportunity for you. We can even hitch up the mules and drag one of the cabins from over here to one of the fields over yonder, if that suits any of you.

"You women and young'uns working in the house or the fields, or helping out around the farm, you can continue to do that. As I said, I cannot at this time pay you wages, and don't know when I can, but there will be food on the table and a roof over your heads as long as you want it. Jane will try to put together some real schoolin' for those who want it. It is up to you."

With that, he returned to the house so his former slaves could contemplate their futures and decide how they wanted to pursue their destinies. He was no longer their problem. Now, he couldn't help feeling, they were his.

Charlie and his son Ned's family opted to farm a portion of Montraville's landholdings not far from the main house, close enough for the mule team to drag the cabin they had been occupying onto that parcel. Ned would be trying his hand at growing corn and other vegetables on the flatlands and, later, tobacco on the hillier section. Montraville gave him the same deal he gave Peters. Two-thirds of the crops would be his.

Sukey came up to Montraville the following day and said: "Massa, if'n I stays put here I reckon I won't never ken what freedom is." She and her two children headed north. She had relatives there who had escaped the South and with their help, eventually, after great difficulties, settled in Atlantic City, New Jersey, working in the United States Hotel at the booming resort town. All three were working there when one of their liberators, Ulysses S. Grant, visited in 1874.

A recent arrival, Amos, had taken up with Rachel from a neighboring farm, and they decided to try their luck in Tennessee. Amos had had numerous disagreements with Montraville, and had shown a penchant for talking back to him, which resulted in a couple of whippings. But he had shown a great aptitude for blacksmithing and decided to try to find work near a Union garrison. They and the rest of those who left in search of opportunities they could only have dreamt of five years earlier were supplied with food and spare clothing.

Another recent arrival, 22 year old Christopher, who had learned his letters, mostly on his own but also with surreptitious help from Jane, became the new foreman, with the understanding that he would assist in the effort to find more hands. He would soon wed Easter, now working mostly in the kitchen. Their wedding, in the Methodist church, celebrated by Montraville, was an occasion to remember.

George, Montraville's former overseer, who now seemed too old and infirm to do much of anything, elected to stay put. He would help take care of a toddler who had been orphaned when his mother, a lively, spirited girl of 17, was found drowned in the creek after being set upon by individuals who were never identified. George and the boy would go on to form a bond that would be broken only when George, seemingly rejuvenated by his new undertaking, passed away many years later.

17

"Saving the Day"

Saving the day for Buncombe County and the rest of the region after the War Between the States can be expressed in four words: education, tobacco, health, and railroads.

It has been estimated that, at the close of the war, at best 10% of the black population in the entire United States could read and write. The percentage in the South was no doubt much lower, since except in rare cases slaves received no education.

The demand for schooling from both black and white children was great, but, it is said, the demand, the clamoring for education from emancipated slaves startled their former "owners," their backers, and government officials. The Freedmen's Bureau and the American Missionary Association provided some teachers and facilities, but there were very limited opportunities in the mountains. For whites as well as for Blacks it must be said.

The North Carolina legislature in 1869 authorized State aid for public schools. And in 1877 re-elected Governor Zebulon Vance had urged the General Assembly to provide for a "normal" school to educate black teachers. He noted that the desire of Blacks for education "is an extremely creditable one and should be gratified as far as our means will permit...." and it was the government's "...plain duty to make no discrimination in the matter of public education." Of course, it didn't happen. Resources were slow in coming, especially for black schools. No State assistance was provided for schools until 1899.

There were no public schools in Buncombe County until 1887. In Asheville there had been private schools, academies of a sort, for white children. After the war, Trinity Chapel and Shiloh A.M.E. Zion Church began offering classes in literacy to black children. And in 1875, Reverend L. W. Pease and his wife Ann, after relocating from New York, converted a livery stable near the center of town into a boarding and day school for black children: the Colored Industrial School, teaching horticulture, agriculture, industrial arts, and domestic labor.

One of the children educated at Trinity Chapel was Isaac Dickson, who, during the campaign for a tax-funded public school proposal in 1887, rallied the support of the black community, which provided the decisive votes in a 722-718 victory. The roll-out was far from pretty. There were constant difficulties. The facilities for white students were poor; those for black students simply inadequate. There were more white teachers, teaching white youngsters, than black teachers, and they were better paid. But it was a step forward that needed to be taken for the area to prosper.

Meanwhile, in the Reems Creek area there was strong sentiment among the inhabitants for education. In the 1830s, an old log schoolhouse had been built near Montraville Weaver's home, attended by the best and the brightest boys and young men in the area. The instruction, by a Mr. Wood, tended to be inconsistent, but it was a start.

Twenty years later education began to hit its stride in the area when a Masonic and Temperance Hall was constructed by the Reems Creek Division Sons of Temperance (the president of which was John Siler Weaver) with a schoolhouse that became the Sons of Temperance High School. Its location was described at the time as "one of the most moral and prosperous settlements of western Carolina...everything [being] of an inviting nature to those who may wish to educate their sons and daughters."

The new high school's principal was James Americus Reagan, who had married Mary Ann, Montraville and Jane's first child, three years earlier. "Competent Female teachers" would assist the principal, governing in a "firm, yet mild and parental" manner. Tuition ran from $5 to $8 per semester and board with "the best families in the settlement" was available for $1 a week, "wood, light and room included; and washing at 37 1/2 cents per dozen pieces."

Then after the war Dr. Reagan decided that a college building should be erected. And since he was married to Montraville Weaver's daughter, and Montraville owned much of the land thereabouts, he knew whom to call on.

"Mont, this community and church are progressing nicely. But we can do even better. And there is one thing we must do to make this area thrive and provide opportunities for our young people. We need a college."

"James, I totally agree, and have been thinking about this for quite some time myself. Just the other day I was talking to John Siler and Jane's brother about the matter. I know they are committed to doing whatever is necessary to create a college. In fact, we decided to form ourselves into a little committee to get this going. I'm assuming you will join us?"

"I cannot tell you how happy that makes me. Yes, I will join you."

"I think we can count on plenty of support from the church and the folks hereabouts. It will be expensive," noted Montraville. "But John, Bill and myself are ready to contribute."

"As am I, certainly, as am I," replied James.

"And we have found just the spot, centrally located, but away from the stands and taverns that might tempt the students. A nice, healthy, Methodistic location. It makes the most sense to put the building near the camp ground so those students who need boarding can be accommodated. I have a parcel near the creek that I will be more than happy to donate."

And so it came to pass. With the donations of the founders, Montraville Weaver, James Americus Reagan, John Siler Weaver, and William R. Baird, Weaversville College was chartered in December 1873 and on June 24th of the following year the cornerstone for the new building was laid, with Masonic honors and an address by Zebulon Vance. It is said that a thousand people attended the event, witnessing the placement under the cornerstone of a Bible, Confederate bills in $100, $20, $5, and $2 denominations, a copy of the current edition of each Asheville newspaper, the Holston Methodist paper, *The Friend of Temperance*, a North Carolina $2 treasury note, and the charters of the area Masonic lodges.

Dr. Reagan became the first president of the college. Latin and Greek, mathematics, natural philosophy, natural and general history, and English literature were part of the curriculum and, given "the demands of female education," there would be "painting, drawing and music." In addition to scholars, the college taught future public school teachers. The college catalogue noted that: "It is a point seriously to be questioned whether the great universities are entitled to that pre-eminent superiority they so pretentiously claim which disdain and ignore the necessity and importance of teaching."

One visitor was in raptures after witnessing an early commencement ceremony: "We almost wished ourselves young again that we might ask admission into their college among these bright-eyed boys and girls, one hundred or more in number, and here to delve for knowledge in this lovely Reems Creek valley, surrounded by gigantic and sublime old mountains on all sides. The selection is a lovely one — just the right place for a large and flourishing college."

To ensure the highest morals were upheld, young men and young women were separated, and the school's charter required that "spirituous liquors shall not be sold within two miles of the institution."

People began calling the community Weaversville, in acknowledgement of Montraville's generosity, and within a couple of years the legislature had officially incorporated the Town of Weaversville, later changed to Weaverville, and Dr. Reagan became the town's first mayor.

The town was now thriving. There were prosperous farms, new shops, a good hotel, a woolen mill, even a base-ball team, which that year routed the team from Asheville in a challenge match 66-43.

*   *   *

In 1869, Samuel Shelton, settling in Chunn's Cove, found that the area's soil, elevation, dry days, and cool moist nights produced the finest tobacco. Seemingly overnight, bright leaf tobacco was introduced to western North Carolina, quickly becoming the area's chief crop. It was much more commercial than the corn which had been the staple for decades, but which was no longer in demand due to the decrease in the drover trade on the Buncombe Turnpike. Tobacco was highly profitable and, what's more, easy to grow. And there was plenty of the hilly, sloping, deeply forested land that now could be used in growing it and in providing the wood needed for curing.

Rough-timbered, square, gabled tobacco barns sprang up everywhere. Once harvested the tobacco could be air-cured in three to twelve weeks. But the more involved flue-curing method, which yielded a more flavorful product, quickly took over. Metal pipes transmitted heat from the continuously maintained, wood-devouring fire into the barns where bundled tobacco was hung.

In any event, by the following year, thirty thousand pounds of tobacco was produced in Buncombe County. Twenty Blacks, four of whom grew tobacco, owned farms. But tobacco was always a sideline for black farmers, whether they owned their farms or were sharecroppers, and by 1880, when 475 thousand pounds of tobacco was produced, the number of black farmers was already in decline as more and more Blacks entered the health and tourism industries.

On Montraville's farm, it was the hottest part of a hot September in the middle of the 1870s, but he shrugged it off as if he were the young man who had just taken over the responsibilities of the farm from his father decades before. He was still the man who, it had been remarked, "labored with his own hands like a slave."

Montraville planted in late May or early June, and was able to cut his crop in September. Today he was checking to see if the harvesting of those valuable leaves should commence.

Most tobacco farmers were harvesting by simply cutting off the stalks at the base and pushing the leaves down over a stake, then letting them dry for a few days. The plants appeared from some distance much like an immense army encampment, with thousands of miniature tents, their sides drooping from their tent pole-like stakes, nestled close together.

But Montraville was using a more difficult method, recently taken up by a few growers, that was highly labor intensive and, frankly, grueling and time-consuming to boot, but which obtained much better results. Instead of severing the stalks with the curved blade of the sickle, single leaves were cropped off the stalks as they ripened.

Since the plants ripened from the bottom up, Montraville was inspecting the plants to determine whether or not enough ripening had occurred toward the base of the stalks to begin the harvest. He wanted to get started because it would take several passes through the fields to complete the harvesting of all the leaves on all the plants. And there was always the prospect that a heavy rainstorm could destroy a tobacco crop in a flash.

Today, he liked what he saw. The so-called "sand lug leaves" at the bottom, those that became soiled from dirt splashed on them during rains, were ready for cropping, as were the leaves directly above them. He would head back to the main house to report to Jane that it was time to assemble a crew to start the harvest.

Of course, harvesting was only the beginning of the process. The tobacco would have to be strung together, hung from poles, and cured. Montraville's "baccer barn" was a recent addition to the farm. Flues ran from a firebox throughout the small structure, heating the air to gradually increasing temperatures, without any exposure to smoke.

When the curing had been accomplished, Montraville would market his crop through an agent in Marshall, D. F. Davis, who by 1879, was handling some thirty tons of tobacco annually. That was when Asheville's first tobacco market, the Pioneer Warehouse, was established. But Montraville tended to avoid the Asheville markets, even as more and more sprang up. Marshall was not much farther and he did not like the coarse language and manners of the Asheville tobacco auctioneers, who would stand outside the markets chanting and haranguing anyone they thought might be selling tobacco, promising the quickest sales and highest prices, which in fact seldom materialized.

When Montraville first started growing tobacco, he had bartered some of his crop and sold the remainder to roving tobacco company buyers. The profits were small. Now, the income from tobacco had overtaken all other agricultural endeavors in the region for most of the large farms. And with it property values were on the rise. It seemed to be a win-win situation, but at the expense of the hillside forests and, as it would later become clear, the health of those who chose to smoke.

*   *   *

Health was also a major factor in the economic growth of Buncombe County and its inhabitants. It had all started centuries earlier with the springs near the Tennessee border, in what became Madison County. Red Bird had once told Montraville tales of the therapeutic powers of the 100 plus degree mineral water springs and the healing ceremonies that had been held at nearby Paint Rock. The springs were regarded as sacred, a connection to the Middle World, and were so important to the Indians that the area around them was designated as "neutral," in other words a sanctuary where the members of any tribe suffering from an illness could go to recover.

However, when, during the War of Independence, two scouts, Henry Reynolds and Thomas Morgan, serving Capt. Benjamin Logan as guards against Indians allied with the British, came upon the springs, it meant that before long the Cherokee and other Indians would no longer have access to them.

It is said that Reynolds and Morgan were chasing after some horses along the French Broad River near what would later become known as Spring Creek when they stumbled into a natural hot tub. The word spread and soon, even before the war ended, curiosity seekers and desperate people pursuing cures for whatever ailed them arrived. By 1788 there was a tavern, then houses, then suddenly a community. Three years later, William Nelson bought the springs for 200 pounds Virginia currency and the tavern became a hotel. By the beginning of the 19th century it had become a well-known spot for rest and recuperation, favored by many illustrious folks, including Bishop Asbury, who noted: "Nelson treated me like a minister, a Christian, and a gentleman."

In 1828, the Buncombe Turnpike was completed. Shortly thereafter James Patton, recognizing an opportunity, bought the springs and began construction on the immense and luxurious Warm Springs Hotel. After Montraville and Jane's son John was born, they had paid a visit to the hotel to assist in Jane's recovery.

Taking the Warm Springs Road, which could be accessed via a wagon ford across Reems Creek, the Weavers first glimpsed the magnificent structure. "Jane, have you ever seen anything so amazing? I'm not sure I can believe my eyes. Now I see why they call it 'Patton's White House.'"

He was understandably taken aback. There was nothing else like the Warm Springs Hotel for hundreds of miles around. The front of the three story main building was 500 feet long with a colonnade of 13 columns representing the 13 colonies. The beautifully landscaped lawn ran down to the French Broad River.

And of course the service was second to none. Patton was highly selective in his staff, including the many slaves that made the day-to-day operation of his establishment possible: chambermaids, waiters, cooks, gardeners, bellmen, teamsters, etc. Slave auctions occasionally held on the premises provided a ready pool of workers for the hotel and it would not be surprising if most of the black men and women, and children for that matter, who ended up with James Patton as their master accepted their fate with resignation. At least they would not be toiling in the fields. And after the war, those who so desired would have the opportunity of paid employment there.

Whether or not any of this might have been off-putting for Patton's northern guests, if indeed any of them noticed, is hard to say. At any rate, it would not have troubled Montraville and Jane.

"The first thing I am going to do," said Jane, "is get into one of those mineral baths they talk about. I can just imagine feeling that warmth."

"Excellent idea, dear. I'll wait for you in the billiard room."

"You will not! You will come with me. It is high time you had a bit of real relaxation."

So after checking in, when they were surprised to encounter young Zebulon Vance, who had recently started working there as a clerk and flower seller, the couple indeed headed for the pool baths and stayed there until it was time for dinner in the 600 seat dining room.

Montraville Weaver was not one to spend a great deal of time resting and he had experienced some qualms about this trip, which was the first real getaway he and Jane had ever had. But all doubts were removed when he tucked into his first meal at the hotel. It was to his mind (and stomach) quite exquisite. Jane felt the same, and now she had some qualms of her own. How was she to come anywhere close in her own kitchen to the standard of the hotel food? Would Montraville expect that? She could only be thankful that her children were not there also.

But Montraville eased her concerns: "This food is uncommonly good, and different, something to savor and think fondly about when we get back home. But I hope you won't try to imitate it. Promise me?"

Her reply: "That is a promise I will find easy to keep."

The rest of the stay was spent bathing, bowling, boating, and sitting on the immense front porch taking the air, reading, and chatting. And of course, eating! They made the acquaintance of many interesting people, some from hundreds of miles away who had come either to rest and relax, or in the hope of improving various conditions, such as rheumatism, lumbago, neuralgia, gout, liver complaints, and ataxy. The Weavers felt truly blessed not to be among their number, able to simply enjoy the air and water (and food of course) without thinking about how poorly they felt. But in truth they missed the children and felt a bit guilty about being away from the farm. So they were soon on their way back home with lots of happy memories.

It was not just the springs that attracted health-seeking visitors to the area. Among many others, the prominent botanist John Lyon, who in his travels through the southern United States discovered 31 new plants, including mountain fetterbush, came to Asheville hoping to find respite from his consumption. After the completion of the Turnpike, planters from South Carolina came to the mountains in the summers, fleeing the low country's heat, humidity, and mosquitoes, and the malaria and yellow fever that seemed to accompany them.

The real boom, however, came after the War Between the States. The mountains in and around Buncombe County quickly became a destination of choice for those seeking relief from respiratory afflictions, especially consumption, the "white plague," at the time the leading cause of death in the United States. A sanitarium was opened in 1871 in the Forest Hill, later Kenilworth, section of Asheville, a decade before the bacterium that caused the disease was identified. Doctor Horatio Page Gatchell, founder of the sanitarium, asserted that the air pressure in Asheville matched one's venous pressure and that the pine-scented air was restorative.

That establishment was soon followed by the Mountain Sanitarium, whose founder, Dr. Joseph William Gleitzman, touted Asheville's elevation at 2,250 feet above sea level, the "pure, clear, mountain air [which] invigorates the lungs and the system in general, and the moderate, little-fluctuating temperatures." Asheville's summer temperatures were claimed to be on a par with those of St. Paul, Minnesota, with winter temperatures akin to places much farther south.

The first sanitarium to treat black consumptives did not arrive until 1912, the Circle Terrace Sanitarium, established by John Wakefield Walker. It was advertised as "the only institution in the world for the exclusive treatment and care of tuberculosis for colored people."

And in general, medical treatment for the black citizenry after the War Between the States was problematic, one could even say dire. There were traveling black medical men of dubious competency, including so-called "herb doctors" who administered concoctions that often did more harm than good. There were no resident black doctors. Blacks were banned from all local hospitals. But the local Women's Christian Temperance Union chapter did offer some home nursing services to poor people, apparently including Blacks.

The *Asheville Citizen-Times* reported that, in addition to groceries, fuel, medicines and clothing: "Scriptural texts, attached to bouquets; also delicacies and often sweet ministrations of songs and readings...." were provided. This became known as the "Flower Mission" because the women often took flowers on their visitations to the sick and destitute. And soon thereafter the Flower Mission Hospital, later known simply as the Mission Hospital, was established, accepting all patients, including Blacks.

But Blacks were treated in a separate ward in the basement. According to one of the hospital's annual reports:

> Our room and facilities for caring for colored people are totally inadequate. Owing to lack of room for this class of patients, a large number have been refused admission. Total depravity and abject poverty among the colored race appear to increase. It does seem that we owe it to them to care for their destitute sick. The colored man is in no way responsible for being among us. He has entered upon an unequal contest. He is handicapped in his race for the goal of a competent livelihood. We have hoped and dreamed that some of our philanthropists, whose interest and enthusiasm in the future of the colored race have not been dulled by a long residence among us, might build a wing on the Woodfin street side of our present building, part of which could be devoted to the care of the colored folk....

The report also noted that: "No worthy sick white person has been refused admission."

At any rate, what was clearly needed was a black physician. In 1884 an organization of black citizens calling themselves the "Black Hills Highlanders" had set about trying to lure a black doctor to the area, but it was not until 1889 that one settled in Asheville. He was Dr. Reuben H. Bryant, a graduate of Shaw University's Leonard Medical College in Raleigh. Others, including Marcus W. Alston, soon followed, eventually setting up practices in the Young Men's Institute.

Still, the Asheville area was considered a healthy place to visit or reside in if you were white. Mayor Edward Aston in 1880 actively promoted Asheville as a destination for tourists seeking a healthy alternative, especially for those suffering from respiratory illnesses. But even as early as that, residents of the area had become fearful of the consumptives being brought into the area and the potential negative effects on business and property values. There was a notable shift from promoting the region as a health tourism destination to emphasizing its desirability for those healthy and wealthy tourists seeking rest and recreation.

*   *   *

In any event, the biggest savior of the region was the railroad, for its impact on commerce in general and especially on tobacco and tourism. Even many years after the war, railway routes from the east terminated at Old Fort, tantalizingly close to Asheville, little more than 20 miles distant. The terrain was formidable, the steep mountainside presenting a major hurdle to linkage of the railroad with the west. Passengers on the one daily train, which mostly carried goods, arriving at 3:25 p.m. (or more often later), had to disembark and board six-horse stagecoaches for the uncomfortable journey to Asheville.

Work on completing the line to Asheville and beyond had stalled due to financial problems, causing the state to purchase the Western North Carolina Railroad. Labor was another problem. Few were eager to take on the back-breaking and extremely dangerous work involved. But in 1875 this problem was solved by the passage of a law permitting the use of convict labor outside of the prisons.

So when, in 1877, contracts were finally awarded to finish the tunneling necessary to take the line to Asheville, the laborers used were almost entirely black men, with a handful of black women serving as cooks, laundresses, and barracks keepers, for which the state charged the railroad thirty cents a day. They had been sentenced by white juries to lengthy periods for minor infractions, for example, ten years for petty theft, five years for vagrancy. If the supply of workers proved insufficient, the authorities simply rounded up more of the unfortunates and brought them before the courts.

They were forced to work on the railroad from dawn to dusk, six days a week, whatever the weather, clearing trees, forming the track bed and then laying the track, surviving largely on navy beans and corn bread, with occasional treats of biscuits, fat pork, and potatoes. Scores of laborers, nearly ten percent a year, died of accident or disease, or in attempting to escape.

Six tunnels were needed, as well as miles of switchbacks and loops to climb the east slope of the Blue Ridge at Old Fort: there would have to be nine miles of track to cover a distance of less than three and a half miles. Workers had to contend with seemingly impenetrable rock. Breaking it apart required either sledge-hammering or blasting. The latter meant that the men had to drill holes, fill them with a volatile nitroglycerin, sawdust, and corn meal mixture, light dry leaves, and run like Hell. Many did not run fast enough.

Almost as difficult to deal with was the spongy soil, called "white mud," often discovered when the rock had been torn away. It seemed to be without any foundation, resulted in constant wash outs, including the washing away of many of the workers when the heavy rains came, and required continuous reshaping of the railway's route.

The most costly and difficult engineering feat was the 1832 foot Swannanoa Gap Tunnel, which was sledge-hammered through solid granite rock. Victory was declared on May 11, 1879, when the tunnelers, who had been working from both east and west, met. A telegram was promptly dispatched to Governor Vance: "Daylight entered Buncombe County through the Swannanoa Tunnel. Grades and center met exactly."

Although later that same day more than a dozen convict laborers were killed in a cave-in, now there was no serious impediment to the achievement of train service from eastern North Carolina all the way to Asheville. And on October 3, 1880, the first train rolled into the station in the village of Best (named for the new owner of the railroad, William J. Best), just south of the town, which now numbered around 2,600 people. On hand to greet it were train representatives, dignitaries, and a large crowd of interested spectators, including Jane and Montraville.

"Jane, remember that time I hiked up to Praying Rock, above where that great tunnel was dug, to take part in a camp meeting? What an awful climb."

"And didn't you once go to one of those musicales put on by the convict workers?"

"Yes, and I didn't approve of it being on a Sunday, but they were such a miserable lot, who could take issue with them having a little fun? Anyhow, fortunately that is now over with."

"I must confess, I find this railroad a mixed blessing. This will no doubt bring prosperity to a great many people, including my fellow farmers. Think how easy it will be to ship what we grow to market, especially when the lines to Paint Rock and Murphy are completed. However, I can't say that I am altogether pleased with what we will be receiving in return."

"But Mont, think of all the wonderful things that we *will* receive in return. I might even be able to find a fashionable dress."

"That is true, although you need no fashionable clothing. You still look glorious in homespun."

"And you're still the gallant, dear, but I can only think how wonderful it will feel to wear something from New York or Boston made with factory cloth."

"All right, let's not argue. I'm sure more elegant clothes and the like will be a boon, and just think about the books that we will now be able to buy. But also think about the salesmen that will flood in offering all sorts of baubles and doodads we have no need for. And the tourists and all sorts of newcomers wanting to breathe our mountain air. I'm thankful that few will find their way to our little town. Asheville will be unrecognizable in a few short years."

And so it came to pass. Pleasure seekers and health seekers, traders of all sorts, began arriving. It was a time of enormous growth with hotels and boarding houses rising up all over the area. Mountaineers came in search of better opportunities and wound up serving as waiters and dishwashers. Labor was needed to mine feldspar, mica, red marble, and quartz, and to harvest timber. Former slaves and their offspring made gains also as they too were needed to stoke the engine of commerce.

Within ten years, the population of Asheville quadrupled. Montraville was correct, the Asheville and Buncombe County he knew would become unrecognizable. But that was an outcome he would not live to see.

18

"Nobody Lasts Forever"

On September 16, 1882, the bell in the Methodist church tolled seventy-four times, announcing to the community the death of Montraville Weaver. The man who had been described as the "head and front," the "father, grand-father, and great-grand-father of the town," was gone. He was "strong and healthy" to the end, doing "as much labor on his farm as anyone else." But nobody lasts forever.

The news spread quickly, even to those beyond the range of the sounding of the bells. The black-edged death notices were printed and sent far and wide, because this was no ordinary death, or perhaps one should say, no ordinary life.

Neighbors, relations, and friends of the family gathered at the house in what was now officially Weaversville. Everyone sought to be of service and in some fashion was accommodated. They consoled Jane and with her children quietly sang hymns and prayed. They covered the mirrors and stopped the clocks. They did any cleaning of the house that was necessary. They brought food: fried chicken, dumplings, cornbread, poke sallet and sweet potato pie.

They pitched in to wash the body after it was placed on the cooling board and dressed Montraville in the clothes he had preached in for so many years, because death was only a passing on of one's earthly existence in preparation for entrance to a better place, the afterlife in Heaven.

Bascombe made a plain pine coffin for his father's last journey. Mary Ann put silver coins over Montraville's eyes to make sure they were closed, so he could humbly enter Heaven. Because who but God can say anyone is truly worthy of admittance? Kittie laid a cloth dipped in soda water over his face to preserve his calm, untroubled expression for the viewing. Autumn flowers had been brought to the house — ironweed, mountain gentian, monk's hood, coneflowers, and asters. These were arranged by Mattie around Montraville's head.

Will and others having the strength that had in the latter days finally deserted Montraville gathered in the nearby cemetery with picks and shovels to prepare his final resting place.

When he had taken to his bed a few days before, Montraville asked his close friend and son-in-law Dr. Reagan to direct the funeral and provide an oration. And Montraville had another request: that he speak with Jane after he was gone to comfort her and assure her that he would be all right, as would she. Taking Jane's hand Dr. Reagan said: "Jane, this is a great loss for us all, and I know you are heartbroken, but we can take solace in the certainty that this man of God will be spending eternal life with Him."

"James, knowing that his suffering is over and that he has gone to a better place is some consolation, yes, but how I will be able to go on without him, I do not know."

"You must put your trust in the Lord. Walk with Him and He will see you through these hard times."

"I know, I know! And I have so many wonderful children and other kinfolk, and friends aplenty, as you can see. But that cannot stop me from realizing that I will never see him again."

"You will see him again, in Heaven. Hold on to that fact with all your might and it will give you the strength to get through the days to come. Let's have a hymn or two. There is one by Charles Wesley that I know was one of Montraville's favorites. He once told me that Bishop Asbury sang it when he visited Montraville's father."

Ah! lovely Appearance of Death,
Not all the gay Pageants that breathe,
With solemn Delight I survey
In Love with the beautiful Clay,
How blest is our Brother, bereft
How easy the Soul, that hath left
This Earth is affected no more,
The War in the Members is o'er,
No Anger henceforward, or Shame,
Extinct is the Animal Flame,
This languishing Head is at rest,
This quiet immovable Breast

No Sight upon Earth is so fair;
Can with a dead Body compare.
The Corps, when the Spirit is fled,
And longing to lie in his stead.
Of all that could burden his Mind?
This wearisome Body behind!
With Sickness, or shaken with Pain;
And never shall vex him again.
Shall redden this innocent Clay;
And Passion is vanish'd away.
Its Thinking and Aching are o'er;
Is heav'd by Affliction no more.

Dr. Reagan's departure was, in effect and completely unintentionally, the signal to begin the celebration of the life of Montraville Weaver. Those who stayed all night would long remember the singing and praying and swapping of stories, not just about Montraville, but about his father John and mother Elizabeth, and their trip over the mountains, and the camp meetings, the long departed Indians, and the war and the hardships after it was lost. Many folks recounted instances of Montraville's generosity and eagerness to help anyone in need, and of course his preaching.

The dawn on the day of the funeral was suitably muted. But it did not take long for the sun to break through. It was going to be a glorious autumn day. After the coffin was loaded onto the ox-driven wagon, Dr. Reagan and the coffin bearers led the short way from the house on Main Street, through the center of town, to the Methodist church on Weaversville's southern edge.

All in black under her widow's bonnet of heavy crepe with a tarlatan border, Jane followed the coffin, with her children gathered close around her, leading the throng of other relatives and friends who had made it necessary to hold the services in the church rather than in the house, as Jane would have preferred.

After the coffin was placed at the front of the old church, the lid was opened and one by one folks paid their final respects, then took their seats. This took some time, as many felt the need to linger at the body and touch it or say a short prayer. Several children, all on their best behavior, had to be lifted up so they could see into the coffin. Then the family took its rightful place after the long line of other mourners had run its course. Jane, it must be said, bore up well, although it was clear that she would have remained beside her love for much longer (an eternity?) if it had been possible.

Because of the prayers and the hymns and the number of prominent persons that wanted to memorialize Montraville, it was nearly two hours before Dr. Reagan began his eulogy.

After welcoming the congregation and talking about Montraville's good life and deeds, especially in establishing the college, he spent a great deal of time reminding those assembled of their mortality and the need to live their lives in a godly fashion:

"Everyone wants to live a good life, but what is that good life? Is it to wring from our short time on this earth as much pleasure and happiness as possible? No, because that is without doubt a surefire way to injure God, our fellow man, and even, in the end, ourselves. No, because for those who have felt the grace and power and love of God, joy is ever present and fulfilling, and we need to give no thought to what we receive in return."

And he finished by again reminding the mourners of "the exquisite beauty of God's work, including, nay especially, death. Death when it comes to one who, like Montraville Weaver, has fully experienced the grace and power and love of God, and is prepared to answer God's call.

Montraville had no fear of death, he embraced it, he embraced the long-awaited, long-desired completion of his work on this temporal world."

After the bodily shell of Montraville Weaver was carried by the bearers to the grave in the adjacent cemetery, and more prayers were invoked for his soul, the coffin was lowered into the earth and covered up. Later, a headstone was placed there with the fitting legend: "I have fought a good fight. I have finished my course. I have kept the faith."

Jane, supported by her children and grandchildren, and legions of friends, would not join him for more than 17 years. Her headstone reads: "She hath done what she could."

Author's note

Little is known, other than through legend, about many of the characters and events depicted in this work. This note constitutes an effort to separate what is known from what is invented or embellished.

A few minor liberties have been taken with timing and the presence of certain characters at certain times, although the basic historical flow of the events is accurate. Most of the white characters are historically correct, or as historically correct as I have been able to make them.

The Indigenous Americans, except for Chief Junaluska and Chief Bowl, are fictitious. The real Chief Bowl, or Chief Bowles, or Duwali, was born in the Province of North Carolina to a Scottish father and Cherokee mother in 1756. There is conflicting information, but it appears that he became the chief of a settlement called Little Hiwassee in the future Cherokee County and that for unknown reasons he led the first large-scale Cherokee emigration westward. He and his followers never became firmly settled, moving from Tennessee to Missouri to Arkansas and finally Texas. Along the way he had become acquainted with the future president of the Republic of Texas, Sam Houston, who presented the chief with a sword, silk vest, and sash upon the signing of a treaty which granted the Cherokee rights to the land on which they had settled. However, the treaty was never ratified, eventually leading to the Texas-Indian Wars. In the last battle of those conflicts, the Battle of the Neches, in 1839, the chief was shot from his horse and killed while wielding the sword that President Houston had given him.

The Blacks, other than those mentioned in Chapter 17 and Easter and Mingo, the latter to the extent that a wanted advertisement proves that he was a slave runaway from Montraville Weaver, on the other hand, are fictitious.

There is much uncertainly about John Weaver's origins, service in the War of Independence, and journey south where he met Elizabeth. The same can be said about Elizabeth's background, including how old she was when she married John. John and Elizabeth's journey with Jacob over the mountains (including the wild hogs and the snowstorm), their settling into the Reems (then Rims) Creek valley, their relations with the Cherokee, their embrace of Methodism, and the life and untimely death of Mr. Rims, which may have occurred before the Weaver's arrival in the area, and the tale of the Yankee bear, are loosely based on popular legend with a more or less factual basis. In any event, the actual circumstances of the Weavers' settling into the Reems Creek area, their homestead and farm, etc., I believe are consistent with life in that area at that time.

Although it is reasonable to suppose that Bishop Asbury visited John Weaver's house, there is no evidence that Montraville met the bishop, or that he recited a Bible verse for him; however, the details about Methodism in general and in Buncombe County specifically are, I believe, accurate.

It is true that Montraville courted and married Jane Eliza Baird, but the story of their courtship and marriage is largely fictitious. The circumstances of John's death and the birth of Mary Ann are fabricated, although John's will is quoted verbatim.

The description of the events of Montraville's youth and relations with the imagined Red Bird are fictitious, but the representation of Cherokee culture and details such as the stickball and other games are factual. The same can be said about what came to be called the Trail of Tears, when approximately 16,000 Cherokee were rounded up and forcibly relocated. (And it should be noted that more than 80,000 Indigenous Americans from other tribes were removed from their homelands during the period.)

That any Cherokee neighbors might have escaped the area just prior to Indian Removal with or without the help of the Weavers is of course conjectural. There may have been Indigenous Americans left in the area by the time of the Trail of Tears. John E. Ross notes that family histories from Bent Creek tell of Cherokee neighbors. And both Cherokee and Catawba were found in Buncombe County later, but not in well-established settlements. At any rate, many Cherokee in western North Carolina did flee to and hide out in the mountains in and after 1838.

The Weavers were heavily involved in the local temperance movement, and there was at least one meeting held on Christmas when testimony was given, committees were organized, and pledges made, but otherwise the goings-on at the meeting described, and Mr. Biggs' "testimony," are a figment of the author's imagination.

The short story printed under the byline of Jane Weaver in the *Asheville News* on January 9, 1851, is quoted verbatim. However, it must be admitted that there is no proof that Montraville's wife Jane was the author of the piece. The only thing for certain is that a woman named Jane Weaver was a prolific short story writer during the 1840s and 1850s with numerous stories published in many newspapers and magazines. So in the chapter in which she is thrilled to learn that her story had been published and reads it aloud to Montraville and the children, this author is exercising some poetic license to which he is sure she would not object. Besides, he really likes the story!

The Abraham Lincoln quotation in Chapter 9 is a private note or "fragment" written when he was presumably wrestling with his views on slavery.

The chapter relating an attempt by two slaves, Cato and Peter, to run away is the author's imagination of the basis for this actual notice in the March 5, 1842 *Asheville News*: "We learn that two negro men and four horses, belonging to James Weaver, Esq., were drowned in attempting to cross French Broad River, a few miles below the Warm Springs, on last Saturday."

The same can be said of the raid on the local farms during the War Between the States, which received a brief, sketchy mention in the same newspaper on April 7, 1864: "A party of fifteen or twenty armed men visited the Reems Creek settlement, eight miles north of this place, on Sunday night last and forcibly took all the firearms they could find. They visited the houses of Rev. Jacob Weaver, Rev. Montraville Weaver, Col. J. T. Weaver, and Capt. Parker. The latter two gentlemen are absent in the service. The band represented themselves as belonging to Col. Kirk's command on Laurel. This may or may not be so. They were pursued by some Confederate cavalry, but made good their escape."

Rev. Coleman Campbell did "make an attempt to have carnal relations" with one of Montraville's slaves, Easter, on the dates mentioned, observed by Montraville, his wife and his son, and this was reported by Montraville to the Methodist Conference, which, presided over by Bishop John Early, expelled Campbell in 1859, but again the details are concocted. However, there is historical evidence of Campbell's talents as a preacher. He was described by Richard Nye Price as

a natural orator, a man of extraordinary imagination [who preached] sermons of considerable eloquence and apparently of spiritual power. In his happiest moods his sermons were prose poems. Had he been a reader and student, he could have established a national reputation as a preacher. But...he was not a student in the strict sense of the word. He read but little; and most of what he learned he gathered from observation, from conversation, and from the sermons to which he listened from time to time.

John Early is another fascinating character. He was described by Price as "the best pathetic anecdoter" he had ever seen.

> He had an almost limitless control over the emotions of his audiences. In the days when shouting was fashionable in the Methodist churches, if quiet and silence were desired, it was unsafe to put John Early in the pulpit....the intense emotionality which made him such a stirring preacher unfitted him for that coolness and calmness of deliberation which the presidency of Holston Conference demanded in that crisis."

A slave named Mingo did run away from Montraville Weaver's farm. Interestingly, in 1866 two former slaves named Mingo Weaver registered pre-Emancipation marriages in Buncombe County. Did Mingo escape and return after the war? Did he abort his escape attempt and return to Weaver's farm voluntarily? Was he captured and taken back to Buncombe County involuntarily, with whatever punishment that may have involved? This we will almost certainly never know. At any rate, other than the fact that Montraville Weaver placed the newspaper advertisement, that chapter is wholly fictitious, although there was a mountain widely, although possibly not officially, called "Nigger Mountain," a reputed hide-out for runaway slaves, the name of which later became "Mount Jefferson." Archibald Thompson, the grandfather of banjo player Dave Thompson, and Archibald's son Avery were freeborn black men residing in the area, although it is not known if they assisted with fugitives hiding on "Nigger Mountain."

The information about New Garden and the men and women of the Underground Railroad in the Greensborough (now Greensboro) area is true, and there was a powerful slaveholder from Jefferson, North Carolina named Colonel George Bower who died attempting to cross a rain-swollen Yadkin River, reputedly while chasing a runaway slave. Further, Dr. Samuel A. Cartwright of Louisiana did invent a mental condition, called drapetomania, which explained why slaves were "absconding from service."

The facts concerning the War Between the States and, for the most part, its aftermath, including those about the founding of Weaversville, or Weaverville, College, the tobacco industry, health tourism and the Warm Springs Hotel, the building of the railway to Asheville, and race relations are I hope accurate, especially including what is said about the military service of the Weaver family. However, most of the details are made up. It is not known if Montraville was working in the tobacco fields toward the end of his life, ever visited the Warm Springs Hotel, or took any interest in the railroad. The letter informing him of the death of Fulton Weaver is quoted verbatim. His eulogy is adapted, in fact largely quoted, from an obituary in the Asheville News written by a fine journalist identified only as "B."

With the exception of Easter and Mingo, the names of the slaves are not known, but their numbers are. In other words, John, Jacob, James, and Montraville owned slaves and where they are described there is a rough approximation of the actual numbers. The attitudes of the Weavers toward slavery in general, and to their own slaves, and the way in which they were treated, are unknown, but I believe in line with contemporary views of slavery in western North Carolina.

The funeral of Montraville Weaver was imagined, although the words on his and Jane's headstones are true. The hymn that might have been sung at the behest of Dr. Reagan, excerpted herein, was composed by Charles Wesley in 1767.

Finally, all the dialogue is invented. Montraville's address to the temperance meeting and Dr. Reagan's eulogy at Montraville's funeral are adapted from various sources. Where there is other quoted material it is quoted verbatim.

A note about Dr. Reagan, preacher and, as indicated, the husband of Mary Ann Weaver, and the first president of the college (and first mayor of Weaversville). He was also a physician and surgeon, and he opened the first pharmacy in Weaversville, where he sold his "New Liver Pills," 25 in a box, 25 cents a box, "superior to any that can be found in the market for all derangement of the Liver, Headache, Indigestion, Costiveness, Billiousness, etc." The pills were endorsed by none other than Governor Zebulon Baird Vance and Senator Augustus Summerfield Merrimon.

Acknowledgments

Many works were consulted in the writing of this book, the most significant of which include "A Lot of Bunkum," the Old Buncombe Genealogical Society newsletter; William Hutson Abrams, Jr., "The Western North Carolina Railroad 1855-1894;" Katie Algeo, "The Rise of Tobacco as a Southern Appalachian Staple," *Southeastern Geographer*; various issues of the *Asheville Citizen-Times* (especially the columns of Rob Neufeld) and earlier Asheville newspapers: *Asheville News, Asheville Weekly Citizen, Asheville Daily Gazette,* and *Asheville Times,* as well as Hendersonville's *French Broad Hustler*; M. Margaret Beal, "The Underground Railroad in Guilford County;" Ora Blackmun, *Western North Carolina: Its Mountains and Its Peoples to 1880*; John Anthony Caruso, *The Appalachian Frontier – America's First Surge Westward*; Cherokee.org website; Elmer T. Clark, "Methodism in Western North Carolina;" Walter Clark, *Histories of the Several Regiments and Battalions from North Carolina in the Great War 1861-1865*; Alice Taylor Colbert, "Cherokee Adaptation to the Ideals of the American Republic;" Amy Duernberger, *Exploring the Southern Appalachian Balds;* Durwood Dunn, *The Civil War in Southern Appalachian Methodism*; John Early, *Diary of John Early*; John Ehle, *The Road*; Brenda Fullick, "Union Troops Sack Asheville," *Mountain Express*; Chris Hartley, *Stoneman's Raid*; S. M. I. Henry, "Temperance Doxology;" Brian Hicks, *Toward the Setting Sun, John Ross, the Cherokees, and the Trail of Tears*; John C. Inscoe, *Appalachians and Race: The Mountain South from Slavery to Segre-*

gation; Inscoe and Gordon B McKinney, *The Heart of Confederate Appalachian Western North Carolina in the Civil War*; Gloria Jahoda, *The Trail of Tears*; Hollis Moody Long, *Public Secondary Education for Negroes in North Carolina*; Nell Pickens, *Dry Ridge – Some of Its History, Some of Its People*; Minutes of the Annual Conferences of the Methodist Episcopal Church; Phoebe Ann Pollitt, *African-American and Cherokee Nurses in Appalachia, a History 1900-1965*; Richard Nye Price, *Holston Methodism – From Its Origins to the Present Time;* Minnie Brank Roberts, unpublished memoirs; Blanche R Robertson, "Some Early History of Rims Creek Valley," Biffle Researchers home page; John E. Ross, *Through the Mountains, the French Broad River and Time*; Forster A. Sondley, *Asheville and Buncombe County*; Hal T. and Muriel G. Spoden, "Sycamore Shoals State Park Historic Area," *Tennessee Historical Quarterly*; Melanie Stories, *The Dreaded 13th Tennessee Union Cavalry;* William K. Thomas, *Bishop John Early*; Mary V. Thompson, *"The Only Unavoidable Subject of Regret," George Washington, Slavery, and the Enslaved Community at Mount Vernon*; Gary Trout, "Our Visitors from North Carolina: Historical Notes on Isle of Wight County Virginia;" Darin J Waters, "Life Beneath the Veneer: The Black Community in Asheville, North Carolina from 1793 to 1900," UNC dissertation, 2012; Pearl M. Weaver, *The Tribe of Jacob*; and Carolyn Whitaker, "Welcome to My Family's History," rootsweb.com. Of great assistance was Jan Lawrence and the Dry Ridge Museum in Weaverville; as well as the North Carolina Room at the Pack Library in Asheville; Les Reker and the "A Fountain of Youth in the Southern Highlands" exhibit at the Rural Heritage Museum in Mars Hill; the Special Collections at the Ramsey Library, UNC Asheville; and "Appalachian Sampler" and Tom Sanders' "The Cherokees" classes at the Osher Lifelong Learning Institute, UNC

Asheville. But it goes without saying that any errors or misrepresentations on the author's part are his responsibility.

CPSIA information can be obtained
at www.ICGtesting.com
Printed in the USA
LVHW111556301122
732981LV00002B/13/J